Tales of a SIXTH-GRADE MUPPET

WHEN PIGS FLY

Story and Art by **KIRK SCROGGS**

LITTLE, BROWN AND COMPANY
New York Boston

Little, Brown and Company

Hachette Book Group
237 Park Avenue, New York, NY 10017
Visit our website at www.lb-kids.com

Little, Brown and Company is a division of Hachette Book Group, Inc.
The Little, Brown name and logo are trademarks of Hachette Book Group, Inc.

The publisher is not responsible for websites (or their content) that are not owned by the publisher.

First Edition: May 2013

Library of Congress Cataloging-in-Publication Data

Scroggs, Kirk.
Tales of a sixth-grade Muppet : when pigs fly / story and art by Kirk Scroggs.
— 1st ed.
p. cm. — (Tales of a sixth-grade Muppet ; 4)
Summary: "Sixth-grade-boy-turned-Muppet Danvers Blickensderfer travels to outer space to learn how he can become human again"— Provided by publisher.
ISBN 978-0-316-18316-1 (hardback)
[1. Schools—Fiction. 2. Space flight—Fiction. 3. Muppets (Fictitious characters)—Fiction. 4. Humorous stories.] I. Title.
PZ7.S436726Tat 2013
[Fic]—dc23
2012040966

10 9 8 7 6 5 4 3 2 1

RRD-C

Printed in the United States of America

Book design by Maria Mercado

To JG and the real Blickensderfer!

Special thanks to

Steve Deline; Joanna Stamfel-Volpe; Jim Lewis and his band
of merry Muppets; Andrea Spooner; Danielle Barthel; Diane, Corey,
Charlotte, and Candace Scroggs; Harold Aulds; Camilla and
Marisa Deline; Joe Kocian; Mark Mayes; Alejandra Arellano;
Jessica Bardwil; Debbie McClellan; Dominique Flynn; Jessica Ward;
Shiho Tilley; and the Disney crew—woo-hoo!

And a special intergalactic space-hog salute to Erin Stein,
Maria Mercado, JoAnna Kremer, Wendy Dopkin, David Caplan,
Hallie Patterson, Erin McMahon, and the Little, Brown crew. Yaaaaaay!

My Life as a Muppet
by Danvers Blickensderfer

If there's one thing I've learned since my Muppetmorphosis, it's that being a Muppet is incredibly complicated. You might not think so by looking at someone like Pepe...

but there are both advantages and disadvantages to my condition.

What do you mean by that, okay?

Great Things about being a Muppet

Chill out, dude! I don't want no trouble!

Hola, ladies! Is it getting hot in here or is it just me, okay?

Fabric Softener can take ten years off your appearance.

Paste on black, furry eyebrows and no one will mess with you.

Girls automatically think you are cute.

Not-so-Great Things about being a Muppet

Sorry, Kid. You only weigh four pounds.

You call that playing basketball?

I've seen better dribbling on baby bibs!

Ha! Ha! *Ha!*

Makes it very difficult to qualify for the school wrestling team.

Opening pickle jars is a challenge with scrawny muppet arms.

Enduring Statler's and Waldorf's insults can wear you out big time.

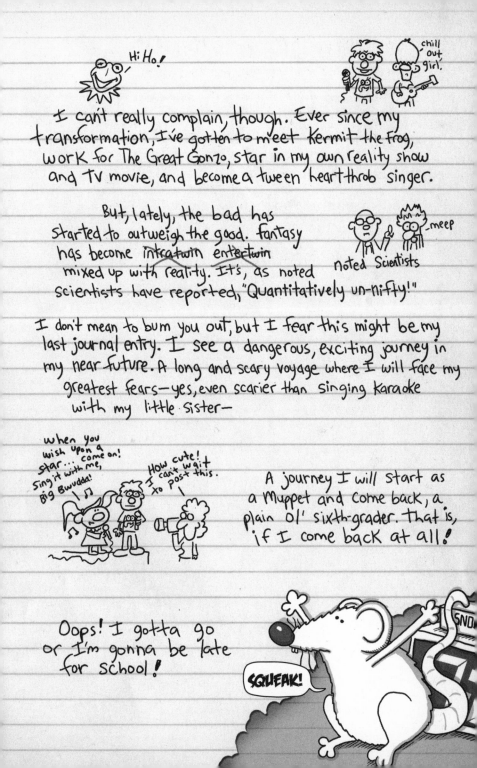

"Hi Ho!"

"chill out girl."

I can't really complain, though. Ever since my transformation, I've gotten to meet Kermit the Frog, work for The Great Gonzo, star in my own reality show and TV movie, and become a tween heartthrob singer.

But, lately, the bad has started to outweigh the good. Fantasy has become ~~intra~~twin ~~enter~~twin mixed up with reality. It's, as noted scientists have reported, "Quantitatively un-nifty!"

Noted Scientists

-meep

I don't mean to bum you out, but I fear this might be my last journal entry. I see a dangerous, exciting journey in my near future. A long and scary voyage where I will face my greatest fears—yes, even scarier than singing karaoke with my little sister—

"when you wish upon a star... come on! Sing it with me, Big Bwudda!"

"How cute! I can't wait to post this."

A journey I will start as a Muppet and come back, a plain ol' sixth-grader. That is, if I come back at all!

Oops! I gotta go or I'm gonna be late for school!

SQUEAK!

SNO

Prepping for a journey into the unknown was gonna have to wait. I had scarier things to face—like my first day at Eagle Talon Academy!

My morning started like any other.

First, I lumbered out of my bedroom at 7:04 AM like a zombie with lead weights in his shoes.

I accidentally cranked the cold knob in the shower.

My pet rat, Curtis, helped comb my feathery 'do while I brushed my teeth.

It was in mid-comb on this particular morning that Curtis suddenly started to squeak wildly, pointing at my face. I hadn't seen him get this bent out of shape

since I swapped his Sassy Rat Rodent Food for Farmer GreenSpleen's Gluten-Free Soy Pellets.

"What is it, boy?" I asked the little squeaking furball. Curtis continued to flail, Kermit-style, pointing at my face.

I leaned in over the bathroom sink and looked at my reflection in the mirror. "I think I look pretty good," I bragged, stroking my chin. "Even got a little manly fuzz growing on the ol' upper lip, right under my—"

The center of my face was as barren as the Mojave Desert. "It's gotta be around here somewhere!" I cried, frantically searching the bathroom floor and then my bedroom: under the covers, beneath the pillow, even in the toy box (my nose has come in handy in several game-play situations).

My nose was nowhere to be found. I turned a suspicious eye to my beloved rat. "Curtis? Did you eat my nose?"

Curtis has been known to enjoy the stuffing in my mom's couch, and I've caught him nibbling on my felty toes a few times. I think he mistook them for sour orange gummy strips. Curtis gave me a huffy *squeak!* and turned away from me, deeply offended. Maybe I had gone a little too far, but suddenly finding that your nose has gone AWOL can make you say crazy things.

Then something occurred to me. I hadn't checked the most likely source of my predicament—the Queen of the Vile, Little Miss Evil, that devil in a pink polka-dot dress: my little sister, Chloe.

Her bed was empty, though, and neatly made, with one of her frightening Fluffleberry dolls sitting on it, watching me with its grinning bug eyes.

I wrapped my head in a long bandage to hide my missing sniffer and headed to breakfast. As usual, when I arrived at the dining room table, I had to turn down a generous breakfast offer from Mom.

"What's up with the bandage, kiddo?" asked my dad, who was flipping through the newspaper.

"Oh, you know," I said. "I...uh, got a pimple on my nose the size of an Antarctic weather balloon. I'm too embarrassed to even show my face. I'm thinking maybe I should just stay home today and call off this whole enrolling-in-a-new-school business."

"I'm thinking maybe you're talking crazy," said my dad, calmly. "After all, your pop is starting his new second job today so you can go to Eagle Claw Academy."

"It's Eagle *Talon* Academy," I corrected him. I did really have an uneasy feeling, and it wasn't just the Sugar Bombs dissolving the top layer of felt off my tongue. Part of me wanted to change my mind, cancel enrolling in Eagle Talon, and run to the safety and mind-numbing boredom of Coldrain Middle School. But I fought those negative, cowardly feelings just as I fought the urge to heave up tingling blue-raspberry cereal milk.

My first order of business was still to figure out the mystery of my missing honker. I looked over at Chloe's seat only to find a single ray of sunshine hitting the empty chair where she usually sat.

"Where's the Angel of Darkness—I mean, uh, where's Chloe?" I asked.

"The movie people picked her up at the crack of dawn," said my mom, sipping her coffee. "Said something about going to shoot at pickups."

"Oh, you mean going to shoot pickups?" I corrected her. "That's where they film extra scenes to help the movie make more sense."

Aha! A breakfast without Chloe. No wonder my mom seemed a little perkier than usual.

Normal Mom   Perky Mom

My little sister, Chloe, was starring in the mega-budget and mega-gag-reflex-testing new movie *Fluffleberries Are Free*. She even missed a few days of school to shoot the movie. Her big Hollywood success irritated me to no end, but it felt almost worth it this morning, since I got to eat breakfast in peace. Chloe is usually full of delightful morning conversation.

My Mornings with Chloe

by Danvers Blickensderfer

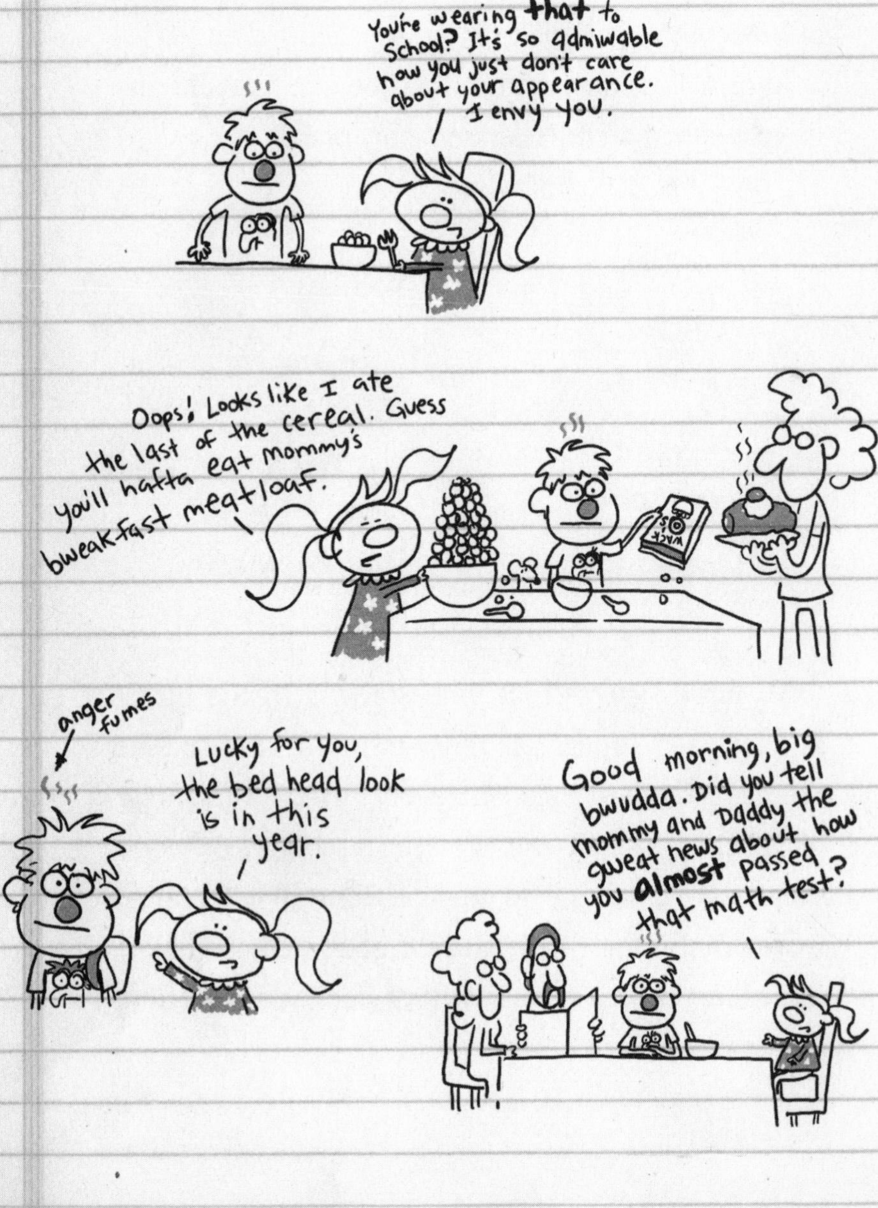

I had no clue as to the fate of my squishy nose and, worse yet, I needed to leave for Eagle Talon in five minutes. I rushed to my room and found a glue stick in Chloe's craft corner.

I tried out an assortment of replacement noses, but nothing seemed quite right.

Cherry Tomato

Pepper Shaker
(very sneezy)

Fresh Strawberry
(attracts ants)

My Mom's Pincushion

Nothing really worked, so I stuck with my bandage. Maybe I could start a new trend—the debonair mummy look.

It was time to go. Curtis gave me a farewell nuzzle and a good luck *squeak!* and I grabbed my backpack and headed out the door.

I felt a little lonely waiting on the sidewalk. It was really weird watching my old school bus zoom by on its way to Coldrain Middle School. I could see my best friend, Pasquale, looking at me out the back window when it passed. He waved at me, and it made me even sadder.

Suddenly, a loud *honk* made me jump. It was my dad in our old, decrepit station wagon. He pulled up beside me, rolled down the window, and announced, "Blickensderfer limo service! All aboard!"

"Dad," I said, getting into the sputtering car, "maybe you should just drop me off a few blocks from the academy—someplace where no one can see this Jurassic clunker."

Yes, sir. This baby can do zero to sixty in... oh wait, actually, I don't think it can go sixty. But it can get pretty close.

I think your car has a sinus infection.

As we pulled into the Eagle Talon Academy parking lot, I guess my dad could see my jittery nerves on display.

"Hey, kiddo," he said. "Don't get spooked. You're gonna do great. And just think, I start my new job at Fried's Circuit Boards today. Imagine—your old man selling computers. I'm the one who should be nervous!"

I couldn't help but chuckle. He had a point. My dad once tried to fix our ancient, outdated, janky family computer with some electrical tape and an oilcan.

DON'T BE SO HARSH. THIS COMPUTER IS DA BOMB, OKAY. SEE, IT EVEN HAS A LITTLE BOMB ON IT.

Principal Sam Eagle's office was colder than a walk-in freezer and full of American flags, statues of buffalo, and portraits of our founding fathers. I stood nervously in the doorway while Sam dabbed paint on a big canvas he had propped up on an easel.

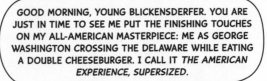

GOOD MORNING, YOUNG BLICKENSDERFER. YOU ARE JUST IN TIME TO SEE ME PUT THE FINISHING TOUCHES ON MY ALL-AMERICAN MASTERPIECE: ME AS GEORGE WASHINGTON *CROSSING THE DELAWARE* WHILE EATING A DOUBLE CHEESEBURGER. I CALL IT *THE AMERICAN EXPERIENCE, SUPERSIZED.*

WOW. THAT'S VERY...UH... PATRIOTIC?

Sam put away his brush, and we sat down at his huge mahogany desk. He suddenly noticed my bandage. "Good heavens! What happened to your face, young man?"

"I...uh...was attacked by angry hornets. Stung me twenty times right on my snout." I should have probably just stuck to my pimple story, but this was getting fun.

"Hmmm," said Sam. "Perhaps you should have Nurse Big Mean Carl take a look."

"You know," I gulped, "I think I'm good."

Sam shrugged and plopped a big stack of paperwork on the desk. "So, today is your first day at Eagle Talon Academy. How are your nerves holding up?"

"I'm a little nervous," I admitted. "Change is kinda scary."

"Ah, yes," Sam reminisced, looking at an old picture of himself as a hatchling in a big bird's nest. "I remember leaving the nest for the first time. It was terrifying, yet incredibly exciting. Of course, I must admit I don't miss having to eat a steady diet of regurgitated earthworms."

"Chef!" Sam slammed his fist down on the desk. "Must you make your lunch menus in my office? It's very distracting."

While Sam and Chef argued cuisine, I pulled out my notebook and a pen and scribbled, "Note to self: Bring lunch from home."

Sam composed himself and pulled out a file labeled DANVERS BLICKENSDERFER, TRANSCRIPT. "Now let's take a look at your grades from Coldrain Middle School." Suddenly he let out a gasp like a fish deprived of oxygen. "This can't be! I didn't think this was mathematically possible."

This wasn't sounding too good.

"What's the matter?" I asked.

"Young man, I had no idea your grades were so inadequate. This is what I get for letting Crazy Harry be head of admissions."

"My grades aren't *that* bad... are they?" I squeaked.

Sam slapped one wing up against his forehead and said, "Let's just say that if you were a restaurant and got these grades, you'd be shut down for having subversive cockroaches doing synchronized swimming in the creamed-corn goulash!"

"Chef, please!" Sam huffed, then turned to me. "Mr. Blickensderfer, I cannot allow you to enroll with these scores. It is not something I can do in good conscience."

"What if you did it in bad conscience?" I asked.

"I'm sorry. It would not be fair to the other students."

I couldn't go back to Coldrain as a total failure, especially after only one day. I had to convince him to give me a shot. "Please, Mr. Eagle! I'll do anything! It's my dream to get the best training available, taught by my Muppet idols. There has to be a way!"

Sam thought about it long and hard, then opened a big red book. "Well, I suppose we could allow a probationary period. Let's see what it says in the rules and regulations."

IT SAYS HERE THAT BY THE END OF THREE WEEKS, YOU MUST HAVE IMPROVED YOUR AVERAGE TO THE GRADE OF USDA PRIME ANGUS.... WAIT A MINUTE, THIS APPEARS TO BE THE RULES AND REGULATIONS FOR BART'S BUTCHER SHOP.

Sam found a different book and read from it. "Aha! 'If said student can raise his or her average to a B after three weeks, then expulsion will not be necessary.' Well, there you have it. We shall give it three weeks. In that time, you will vigorously study the areas of math and science, your weakest subjects. That's not to say you have any strong subjects."

"Math and science?" I groaned. "I might as well pack my bags for Coldrain right now."

This was just great! I transferred to Eagle Talon to achieve Muppet glory and master the entertainment arts, and now I was facing a three-week mathematical boot camp!

YOU KNOW WHAT THEY SAY, YOUNG MAN: WHEN LIFE GIVES YOU LEMONS, SHAVE OFF THE ZEST, MIX IT WITH ONE EGG, CREAM, AND A LITTLE SUGAR, WHIP IT UNTIL FIRM, AND MAKE LEMON MERINGUE.

WØT DEE HØØEY! DERT IS FRURDAY'S LØØNCHIE SPESHY!

MENÜ
LØØNCHIE SPESHY

DESSØØRT:
LERMONEE
MØØRINGUEY
SLICEE DER
CRÈMEPIE
YUM-YUM!

Fortunately for me, my first class of the day had nothing to do with math or science—it was something much more fun: music appreciation. Sam personally escorted me to class and when he opened the door for me, the place was a madhouse. Kids were laughing, climbing over their desks, tossing paper airplanes across the room—it was a lot like Mr. Piffle's class at Coldrain, only with more bagpipe-playing penguins.

The class froze in terror when they saw Sam.

"Great James Abram Garfield's ghost!" cried Sam. "Children! I demand that you return to your seats and behave this instant!" The kids in the room bolted back to their desks and quieted down. "Now, where is today's guest instructor?" Sam continued.

That's when Rowlf the Dog burst into the room with a loud, "Hiya, folks!"

"Rowlf!" Sam huffed. "I hardly think it's appropriate for a teacher to be late for his own class!"

"Sorry, I'm tardy," apologized Rowlf. "I seem to have overslept."

"Well, now that you're here, I'd like you to extend a warm welcome to Danvers, our newest student," continued Sam. "Rowlf, I trust you will instill the impeccable values and standards Eagle Talon is known for and teach only the classics. None of those wild, uncouth, tasteless sideshow acts that the Muppets have inflicted upon us over the years. No boomerang trout. No samurai birthday cakes. No exploding Koozebanians. I want you to immerse these children in fine art, mold their impression-able minds, and soon they will be bitten by the learning bug."

"Right." Rowlf nodded. "Immerse the children, mold their brains, and they'll be bitten by bugs. This is starting to sound like a bad horror movie."

"This is no joking matter. I expect discipline and results." And with that, Sam left the classroom, slamming the door shut behind him.

"Sheesh, Rowlf!" I said. "I didn't realize you were a strict classical music instructor in your spare time."

"Don't worry." Rowlf smirked and sat down at his piano. "My *Bach* is worse than my bite."

I found an empty seat right in between two familiar faces: my old nemesis, the jokester Phips Terlington, and my fellow Muppet Theater intern Hockney.

Hockney looked flustered and uptight, as usual. "I just want to apologize on behalf of my fellow students," he said. "Normally, this isn't how this class conducts itself."

"Yeah," snarked Phips. "Normally, it's way crazier!" Suddenly, he bolted out of his chair and ran to the classroom door.

Marvin's song was amazing, and the whole class helped out by playing the cymbals, triangle, and xylophone—and some kids just banged their desks with their textbooks. It was awesome. When it was over, the class erupted in cheers as Marvin took a dramatic bow. "Zank you! Zank you! You have been ze best audience since we played ze Lake Oweeyoweee Annual Sledgehammer Convention!"

"I *hated* that gig," added one of the Muppaphones.

Suddenly, from the doorway, Phips Terlington shouted, "Heads up! Sam is coming back!"

Everyone plopped back in their seats, Marvin pushed his Muppaphones behind the curtain, and Rowlf started playing a slow, sad Beethoven tune on his piano.

WHAT WAS ALL THAT RACKET? I COULD HAVE SWORN I HEARD THE ACCENT OF A SILLY MAN WITH A MUSTACHE AND THE IMPACT OF RUBBER MALLETS ON THE CRANIUMS OF ARMLESS, MULTICOLORED FURBALLS TO THE TUNE OF "HAMMER IT ON HOME!"

Rowlf kept a straight face as he played his keyboard. "Not in here, my fine, feathered educator. Check Madame Zelda Rose's accounting class next door. They get a little crazy in there sometimes."

Sam gave us all one last look with a raised eyebrow. "Very well, then. Carry on." And he shut the door.

The class let out a sigh of relief.

I was relieved, too. I was no longer quite as worried about my grades at Eagle Talon. This truly was the place to learn to be all the Muppet you can be.

I CAN'T BELIEVE YOU LET A GUY WHO SMACKS FURBALLS WITH A HAMMER TEACH CLASS.

IT'S WHAT WE CALL THE SCHOOL OF HARD KNOCKS.

OKAY, I'LL DISTRACT HIM WHILE YOU GRAB HIS MALLET.

GRAB HIS MALLET? DUDE, WE DON'T HAVE ARMS.

OH, YEAH.

The rest of my day at Eagle Talon was a breeze, and when the final bell rang, it was time to head over to my after-school internship at the Muppet Theater! I couldn't wait to get there and see Pasquale. Even though it had only been one day, it felt like a million years since I had seen my best bud.

Inside the theater, there was a strange vibe in the air. Everyone was hustling and bustling about, practicing acts, prepping props, painting sets—the usual. But the theater also seemed a little off-kilter. It was like the whole building was slightly swaying and rumbling. Something was different, but I couldn't quite put my finger on it.

I spotted Pasquale over in the corner near the loading dock and ran over just to say "Hey."

"Hey, what happened to your nose?" asked Pasquale.

"A, um, a rabid chipmunk thought it was an acorn and buried it on the playground until next spring."

"You lost it, didn't you," Pasquale said.

"Yep. Can't find it anywhere."

It was so great to see my friend again. We filled each other in on the day's events as if we had been apart for ages.

I told Pasquale all about my crazy Marvin Suggs jam session, my unfortunate grade-point problem, and Swedish Chef's menu monstrosities while he filled me in on the latest news from Coldrain.

Like how he had asked Sofi, his new crush, out on a date.

And how Mr. Piffle had regaled the students with exciting tales plucked from the headlines of history.

And how Coach Kraft had given them valuable self-defense tips in P.E.

"I hate to say it," I told Pasquale, "but I kinda already miss Mr. Piffle's boring lectures and Coach Kraft's torture sessions. They're probably more fun than the math misery Sam Eagle has in store for me."

"Well, don't forget," said Pasquale, "you still have access to the best math tutor in town. And all I require in return is lots of cash and expensive gifts."

"Oh, that reminds me," I said, unzipping my backpack. "I got you a souvenir!" I pulled out a blue T-shirt and held it up. "It's an official Eagle Talon Academy T-shirt. They only had XXL, so I figure you can use it as either a tent or a parachute."

"Awww, you shouldn't have....I mean, really, you shouldn't have. You could fit three of me in this thing." Pasquale smirked and was reaching for the shirt when, all of a sudden—*sploot!* The shirt was sucked away!

"What the?" I jumped. "Where'd it go?"

HA HA! YOU, SIR, ARE NO MATCH FOR THE SCHNOZ-SLINGER!

"Cool outfit, Gonzo!" I said.

Gonzo lifted up his mask, looking a little disap-pointed. "Rats! How did you figure out it was me?"

"Um…let's just say you have a distinctive profile," I said. "What's with the superhero getup?"

"It's part of our new act!" Gonzo beamed. "A stunt spectacular based on America's three thousand and thirtieth favorite superhero!"

I HAVE IT ON GOOD AUTHORITY THAT SUPERHEROES ARE GOING TO BE REALLY BIG THIS YEAR. THEY'RE MAKING A COMEBACK.

SI. AND IN OTHER NEWS, WATER IS GOING TO BE VERY WET THIS YEAR, OKAY.

I took a good look at Gonzo's mask. The snout had a little piece of web hanging from it. "So this is how you snatched that T-shirt so fast."

"That's right," said Gonzo. "Dr. Honeydew and your pal Pasquale actually teamed up to create a snout-firing mechanism that could launch a synthetic polymer fiber three hundred times stronger than a spiderweb! I can fire the web from long distances with just one blast from my nose!" He slipped the mask back on. "Watch this!"

Pasquale pulled me aside and whispered, "Oh, I was wondering, any news on your Muppet-morphosis? Is Dr. Honeydew any closer to solving the mystery?"

"Funny you should ask," I said. "Just last night, I got a call from—"

"Hi, ho and ahoy there, Danvers!" came a voice from behind us. It was Kermit the Frog and Fozzie Bear, and they were decked out in eighteenth-century seafaring duds. For a second I thought it was disco pirate Sunday and I had forgotten to dress up.

Just then, I felt the room sway again, almost like we were on water. And I swear I could hear seagulls outside the window. From The Electric Mayhem

Band's rehearsal space, the sound of pirate songs drifted out and down the hall.

Then, to make matters even wackier, I heard the jingle of sleigh bells.

"Hey, kid!" came a cranky old voice from above.

I looked up to see Statler and Waldorf hanging from wires, dressed as ghosts, with white skin, raggedy clothes, and long, rattling chains.

I looked around at Kermit and Fozzie and the rest of the gang, and no one appeared to think anything was amiss about all this...even Pasquale was taking it in stride.

"*Pardonnez moi!*" said a voice from behind me. "Young beauty queen diva coming through!"

It was Miss Piggy, and she was dressed in a tiara and beauty pageant gown.

THANK *VOUS*! THANK *VOUS*! I PROMISE TO FULFILL MY DUTIES AS MISS BOGEN COUNTY AND ALWAYS REMEMBER THE LITTLE PEOPLE I HAD TO STEP ON TO GET HERE!

DAT'S ME, OKAY.

Piggy sashayed past us, throwing flowers, and waltzed into her dressing room, slamming the door after her.

"Ahem!" I coughed. "Excuse me. Doesn't anyone here think it's a wee bit strange that Statler and Waldorf are made up as ghosts, just like they were in *The Muppet Christmas Carol*? And, Kermit and Fozzie, why are you dressed as your characters in *Muppet Treasure Island*? And Miss Piggy? She was Miss Bogen County in *The Muppet Movie*. Do you really think she's still a young beauty pageant queen? Give me a break!"

"Sorry." I gulped, then turned to the others. "Snap out of it! You're either mixing up fantasy with reality or you're doing some weird memory-lane freakout."

Pasquale shook his head, like he was coming out

of a dream. "Whoa! It's true. This is bizarre. It's like we all momentarily lost our minds."

Kermit and Fozzie took off their hats and costumes. "This is crazy," said Fozzie. "Danvers is right. We're not Captain Smollett and Squire Trelawney, sailing on *The Hispaniola* in search of pirate treasure…"

Then they darted off down the hall, suddenly totally convinced they were the characters they played in *The Great Muppet Caper*.

Pasquale and I were left alone in the hall. All was quiet except for the sound of the floorboards of the theater, creaking and moaning like the planks of a ship swaying on the sea.

Another big rumble shook the building.

"We have to reverse my condition," I said. "Things are getting out of hand. The disruption it caused in the universe is now starting to affect other people—er, Muppets! The effects of my Muppetmorphosis are clearly reaching critical mass."

After finishing our internship work for the afternoon, Pasquale and I stopped by the Snackmart on the corner for some frozen Splershies. I got my usual mix of White Cherry, Blue Raspberry, and Tongue-Imploding Citrus—proven to tickle the taste buds and strip paint off old lawn furniture.

We sat outside on the steps, enjoying our treats.

"Hey! You never finished telling your story," said Pasquale. "You were saying you got a call last night from Dr. Honeydew?"

"Oh, yeah!" I replied. "He called me and went on and on about some green glow from outer space. In fact, he said—Oh, wait! He said he wants us to meet him at this street corner after our internship." I took a look at the clock on my cell phone. "I forgot all about it. Hope we're not late...."

Suddenly, Pasquale and I were grabbed from behind by two dark figures! Our Splershies went sailing as we were tossed through the open doors of a stretch limo. Inside the limo, we found ourselves sitting across from our abductors: Uncle Deadly and Bobo the Bear. They were decked out in black suits and dark shades—the men in black! Or should I say, the bear and the—what the heck is Uncle Deadly, anyway?—in black.

"What kind of kidnappers are these?" Pasquale whispered. "They seem awfully concerned about our well-being."

I decided to stand up to them. "Where are you taking us? I demand to know!"

"I'm afraid it is top secret, young man." Uncle Deadly laughed. "We have been sworn to secrecy."

"Yeah." Bobo nodded. "And we especially can't talk about secret government labs, outer space, or flying to the far side of the galaxy to save the universe from total destruction."

Uncle Deadly smacked Bobo in the shoulder and shouted, "TMI!"

"Whut?" said Bobo.

"Too much information!" snapped Deadly. "You'll ruin everything!"

"I thought TMI was for something gross," said Bobo. "Like talking about how you chew on your own toenails when you're nervous."

Uncle Deadly smacked Bobo again. "That was private information! I told you that in confidence!"

"I wish you hadn't told me at all. I haven't had an appetite since!"

While Deadly and Bobo argued, I leaned over to Pasquale and whispered, "These are the worst secret agents I've ever been kidnapped by."

"These are the *only* secret agents you've ever been kidnapped by," Pasquale pointed out.

"This is true. Maybe we can jump from the moving vehicle. It's going pretty slow."

Pasquale shook his head. "Are you crazy? You're made of felt. Only you can do that kind of thing. I'd be a broken, bruised mess if I tried it."

The car came to a halt with a *screeeeeech!*

We were in an alley behind a big brick building.

"We have arrived at our secret location." Uncle Deadly cackled. "Mwah ha ha ha ha!"

"Uh, dude, I recognize this place," said Pasquale. "This is the back of the Pepperoni Planet Pizza Parlor. I'd know that smell of cheesy bread anywhere." Then he leaned over to me and whispered, "I'm gonna bring Sofi here after our date at the mold museum."

"Curses! Foiled again!" hissed Deadly.

They escorted us out of the limo and in through the back entrance of Pepperoni Planet.

"This place lets us rent out the private birthday room," said Bobo. "It's affordable and looks all futuristic, plus we get fifty free Skee-Ball tokens."

"Just don't tell the kids reading this book," whispered Deadly. "We want them to think it's an expensive military command center."

We stepped up to the special birthday room door.

"Execute the super-secret knock!" ordered Deadly.

Bobo knocked on the door with a bunch of short knocks, long knocks, hard knocks, soft knocks, rapid-fire knocks…sheesh, it went on forever!

Pasquale whispered, "He's knocking to the tune of 'Ninety-Nine Bottles of Beer on the Wall.' We might be here awhile."

Once he was done, we could hear a series of locks and deadbolt mechanisms clanking and turning on the other side of the door before it slowly creaked open. Then computer beeping noises filled the air, and a figure with a shaggy mop top popped out!

Inside the birthday room—I mean, uh, the secret military complex—we found Dr. Bunsen Honeydew and Beaker. And behind them was a large table where Kermit, Fozzie, and Pepe were all sitting! I noticed that Kermit and Fozzie were back to normal—no pirate or reporter gear in sight.

"Welcome, gentlemen," Dr. Honeydew greeted us.

"You know, you really didn't have to send government agents to kidnap us and bring us to Pepperoni Planet," I said. "Just mention cheesy bread and we're here."

"Sorry about that," said Kermit. "We were under direct orders from the publishers to make this book more exciting."

"Would you like any refreshments before we begin?" asked Dr. Honeydew. "A root beer float, perhaps?"

"Sure thing!" I said.

Dr. Honeydew turned to Beaker and said, "Two floats for our guests, Beaker."

"Meep!" chirped Beaker as he darted off, then a split-nanosecond later he appeared next to us with the floats.

HOW DID YOU DO THAT SO FAST?

That's when I glanced around the room and noticed that there were Beakers everywhere! Some were looking over charts, others were operating computer screens, and some were playing Angry Chickens in the corner.

"Hey, Dr. Honeydew," I said. "There's, like, forty Beakers running around this joint."

"Yes, I'm afraid so." Honeydew sighed. "An unfortunate side effect of a glitch with the new copying machine I installed in my lab. It's called the ManyMe LX. It's nice having so many new test subjects, but they're beginning to get unruly. I think they might still be harboring a grudge from the time I used Beaker's nose to test the freezing point of vanilla custard."

Sure enough, the Beakers running around were kind of irritable, and they were giving Dr. Honeydew the stink eye.

I nudged Pasquale. "This is just like *The Muppet Show*, season five, episode fourteen, where Beaker accidentally clones himself and causes utter chaos at the theater."

WELL, LOOK ON THE BRIGHT SIDE. I'M SURE WE'VE ALL SAID TO OURSELVES, "I WISH I HAD AN EXTRA SET OF HANDS."

I HAVE NEVER SAID SUCH A THING, OKAY.

Kermit stood up and called for our attention. "Let's get started. Gentlemen, we have a problem. As you know, months ago, young Danvers here was transformed from a child into a Muppet at 12:22 AM by a mysterious green flash of light. Ever since that night, the world has been breaking down into chaos and becoming unstable. Why, just today, Fozzie, Miss Piggy, and I were running around acting like characters from our movies. Luckily, Dr. Honeydew convinced us to snap out of it, but I'm afraid that if we don't reverse Danvers's Muppetmorphosis, it could tear apart the fabric of our reality. And as any Muppet knows, felt tears very easily."

A rumble shook the building and jostled our root beer floats.

"What was that?" asked Pasquale.

"The fabric of reality tearing apart," I whispered back. "Or maybe a rampaging dinosaur."

"I would now like to invite Dr. Bunsen Honeydew to elaborate on our predicament," continued Kermit.

"Thank you, Mister Kermit," said Dr. Honeydew, projecting a map of space onto a huge screen. "Recently, we picked up on a bright green flash some sixty thousand light-years, twenty-three light-days, and twelve light-minutes from Earth. It was a green flash very similar to the one Danvers witnessed before his Muppetmorphosis. It appears to have originated in the Grand Ol' Galaxy."

"What do you think it could be?" I asked.

"We have irrefutable evidence that it is linked to your conversion," continued Dr. Honeydew. "But how it affected you, so far away on this planet, is a mystery."

I couldn't believe it! Irrefutable evidence! Whatever that meant, it sounded pretty promising. "You've finally done it, Doc," I cried. "You've cracked the case."

"Don't thank me," said Dr. Honeydew, pointing to a computer with spinning tape reels for eyes and bleepy lights all over. "Thank our new supercomputer, HOWIE 5000. HOWIE, of course, is short for Hexadecimal Online Wireless Interfacing Electro-gadget."

Dr. Honeydew walked up and patted the computer on the back, saying, "Weeks ago, we filled HOWIE 5000's databanks with all known information about Danvers Blickensderfer and his transformation, including his personal data, school performance, and pop-music Bigboard Chart history."

"Affirmative," said HOWIE 5000. "I am familiar with every song by Danvers's group, Mon Swoon, and the supergroup that was formed by combining Mon Swoon with Emo Shun, called M.E.S.S., including all extended Euro dance remixes. If I had human emotions, I would classify them as...straight-up dope, yo."

Dr. Honeydew continued, "Yes, well, we then assigned HOWIE the task of processing all that info and solving our mystery using computer technology. Not only did he first spot the green flashes from the wormhole, but he also picked up and recorded sound waves that have been emanating from across space as well. We have brought in a sound expert to listen to those signals."

SORRY, I'M LATE, DOC. I WAS JUST SAYING HELLO TO BEAKER—FORTY-FIVE TIMES. THAT GUY MUST THINK A LOT OF HIMSELF.

Rowlf plugged his headphones into the super-computer and Dr. Honeydew said, "HOWIE, please play back those sound waves for Rowlf."

"You must first insert a quarter," bleeped HOWIE 5000.

"Oh, of course," said Dr. Honeydew, fumbling for change. "HOWIE 5000 was constructed from an old jukebox and snack-machine parts." He inserted the coin and hit PLAY.

IT APPEARS TO MY CANINE RECEPTORS THAT THE FAINT SIGNAL IN QUESTION IS A CATCHY POP DITTY BEING BROADCAST AT POINT-ZERO-ZERO-FIVE DECIBELS. OF COURSE, I'M MEASURING THAT IN DOG *EARS*!

"Affirmative, sarcastic canine creature," agreed HOWIE. "I used my built-in Dooby Stereo modulating components to amplify the signal, remove any distortion, and lay down a phat bass beat. It's quite groovy. Danceable, yet chill."

"Let me listen to that," I said, putting on the head-phones. The audio signal coming out of HOWIE's speaker sounded just like "Girl, Don't Be Rash," the hit poison ivy song I had recorded with my friends Kip and Fozzie and the other members of M.E.S.S.

THAT'S CRAZY! HOW IS OUR SONG PLAYING A MILLION MILES AWAY?

I SHALL TAKE LEGAL ACTION, OKAY! I NEGOTIATED THE FOREIGN RIGHTS FOR PORTUGAL AND CANADA ONLY! THE CONTRACT SAYS NOTHING ABOUT WORMHOLES IN OTHER GALAXIES!

"It's a mystery," said Dr. Honeydew. "But it proves that there is an undeniable link between the wormhole and you. I believe we have to transport you to the site of the wormhole and thrust you back through. Otherwise, we are doomed to utter and complete annihilation...or, at the very least, we will be mildly inconvenienced by a chronic case of the heebie-jeebies."

"Well, then, that settles it," announced Kermit. "We'll have to contact the Space Administration and transport Danvers to that wormhole."

HOWIE 5000 chuckled. "Forgive me for expressing

laughter, naïve amphibious creature. But a trip to the Wormhole N-1 would cost over thirty million billion dollars."

Everyone in the room gasped and dropped their cheesy bread.

Dr. Honeydew gulped. "Oh, dear! I had no idea it would be that costly."

"We will find a way," pledged Kermit.

How were we ever going to come up with that kind of money? It was a long shot, but we just had to make it happen.

hen I arrived home, I was exhausted and just wanted to crawl up to my top bunk and collapse like a piece of soggy broccoli. But as soon as I stepped into the apartment, I was greeted by my folks, looking super-serious and grim. Curtis ran up my pants leg and shirt and clutched my shoulder. I was immediately worried.

"Danvers," said my mom, "I'm afraid we have some shocking news."

I couldn't believe it. What five-year-old gets arrested? "What happened?" I asked. "What did she do?"

"We're not sure," answered my dad. "But if there's a law against being sassy, your sister could be going away for a long time."

We all hopped in the station wagon and headed down to the Block City police station. We parked the car and slowly made our way through the cold cement-and-brick halls, the sound of clanging cell doors and the shouts of criminals echoing off the walls. It was pretty scary.

We ended up at the front desk, where a uniformed officer was stationed. The officer was dozing, his head bobbing up and down. I rang the bell on his desk and he bolted awake, one hand on his nightstick, shouting, "What? Who? Where? Wocka?"

My jaw hit the floor—it wasn't a police officer. It was Fozzie Bear in a policeman outfit!

Fozzie got a look at us and calmed down. "Oh, sorry, folks. I dozed off. We policemen are always exhausted, you know."

WHY ARE POLICEMEN ALWAYS EXHAUSTED?

BECAUSE WE NEED *ARRESTS!* GET IT? A-REST?! WOCKA! WOCKA!

This was no joking matter. "Fozzie," I said. "Why are you dressed like a cop?"

Fozzie gave me a weird look. "I don't know any Fozzie. I'm Bear on Patrol, here to uphold the law and trust the public services...or is it serve the public trust? I miss that one every time on my patrol bear test."

I leaned over to my parents and whispered, "This is really strange. Fozzie is acting like his Patrol Bear character from the old *Muppet Show* skits. He doesn't even recognize us. It's like I've been telling you—fantasy and reality are getting intertwined."

Another rumble shook the police station. I was starting to feel like we lived on a fault line.

My dad stepped up. "Ahem. We're here about Chloe Blickensderfer. We want to bail her out."

"Why? Is she sinking? Wocka! Wocka!" Fozzie laughed. Then he noticed that my dad wasn't smiling and gulped. "Okay. Well then, let me check my roster."

Fozzie flipped through a big binder and stopped. "Here she is—Chloe Blickensderfer. Oh, *her*! Yes, please take her back!"

Fozzie pulled out a huge ring of keys and rushed over to a big metal door. "I'll go get her. Wait here!"

After some clanging around, the door opened

up and Chloe was escorted out, clutching her Fluffleberry.

"We've decided to let her off with a warning because she's so young," said Fozzie, releasing Chloe to my folks. "Plus, she's intimidating the other prisoners."

"But what did she do, Officer?" asked my mom.

"Breaking and exiting!" Fozzie announced, looking at the list of charges. "No, wait—that can't be right. Breaking and entering!"

"We still don't understand what this is all about, Officer," said my dad.

"Maybe I can clear this up," said a strange voice. A shady-looking shark in a bright pink suit with pink sunglasses stepped up and presented his card. "Allow me to introduce myself. I'm attorney Finn Kontempt, lawyer for Fluffle Incorporated. I'm afraid your darling little daughter here isn't the precious angel you think she is."

"Tell me something I don't know," I said.

THIS LITTLE FIEND WAS CAUGHT RIFLING THROUGH TOP SECRET FILES AT THE FLUFFLEBERRY HEADQUARTERS. AND SHE TRIED TO STEAL SEVERAL KEY DOCUMENTS.

My dad looked over at Chloe. "Is this true, young lady?"

"It's all lies!" shouted Chloe. "I've been fwamed! I'll tell you all about it when we stop for ice cweam at Two Scoops of Paradise on the way home."

"I don't think ice cream is in the cards for you tonight, young lady," said my mom. "Now, be honest: Is this the first time you've ever taken something that doesn't belong to you?"

"Of course." Chloe smiled. "Well, there *was* the time I stole some of Danvas's silly boxer shorts and took them to school for show-and-tell."

"You showed my Easter Bunny boxers in class?" I raged. "You are a monster!"

"If you could have seen the tears of laughter on those kids' faces," said Chloe. "You bwought them gweat joy."

"How dare you?" I screamed. "They should have thrown the book at you!"

"Thank you for not pressing charges," my dad told the lawyer. "This will be the last time anything like this ever happens, I promise."

"There is one last thing," Fozzie added. "We did find this squishy, bouncy ball in her pocket." He held up an evidence bag with a red, round object in it. It was my nose!

I grabbed the bag and barked at Chloe, "I should have known you were the one who took my nose! Do you know how humiliating it is to go to school with a missing facial feature? I bet you were gonna sell it online, or at some charity auction!"

"That's a gweat idea," said Chloe. "But no. I needed it to—"

"I don't want to hear it!" I yelled, ripping off my bandage and slapping my schnoz in its proper place. "I'm never speaking to you again!"

I was so fuming mad, I had to go stand in the corner and cool off.

My mom took Chloe by the arm, gently, and said, "Come on, honey. Let's go home."

Chloe was irate. "Handcuffed by cops! Thrown in pwison! Falsely accused! And no ice cweam! This is the worst night of my life!"

IT'S ABOUT TO GET WORSE, SWEETHEART. I'M AFRAID THAT YOU WILL NO LONGER BE IN OUR MOVIE, *FLUFFLEBERRIES ARE FREE.* WE ARE EDITING YOU OUT AND REPLACING YOU WITH A COMPUTER-ANIMATED UNICORN NAMED OUCHY.

OUCHY

CONTRACT

Things at home were pretty tense, at least between me and Chloe. I felt kinda bad for her, what with her Hollywood dreams being shattered and all, but I wasn't ready to be her best bud just yet. Not that we were ever best buds, or even worst buds.

Curtis didn't like it when Chloe and I weren't getting along. He must have thought I wasn't being very nice because he gave me the "talk to the paw" treatment. He had only done that once before, when I gave him mouse treats instead of rat treats. Rats are a proud species.

But I had to stand my ground with Chloe. She couldn't just be stealing my body parts without my permission. Today, it was my nose. What would she take tomorrow? My left foot? My appendix? Oh wait, the doctors took that when I was five, but you get my drift.

* * *

Luckily, things at Eagle Talon Academy were starting to improve. I was making new fuzzy friends, learning all sorts of interesting tidbits and whatnots, and, so far, I had avoided any grueling math and science exams.

In fact, Sam Eagle was really the only one there who made me nervous, and I knew, once he wasn't around, each class would turn into something much more . . . uh, interesting.

The rest of the day sailed by smoothly. After school, Pasquale met me on the way to the Muppet Theater. He was waiting for me near the Snackmart with two fresh Splershies.

"Hey," said Pasquale, handing me my beverage. "How was your day?"

I took a sip and grimaced as the citrus pickled my tongue like sweet gherkin. "It was kind of awesome. I'm not sure if I'm learning anything, but going to class is a lot more fun."

Suddenly, a fire truck, an ambulance, and a police car flew by us with their sirens blaring! They zoomed around the corner with a *screech!*

We dropped our Splershies, and I screamed, "Hey! They're headed toward the Muppet Theater!"

The theater was in shambles! It looked like a woolly mammoth had played flag football through the front lobby. There were chunks of brick, concrete, and fiberglass everywhere, and sparks were shooting from broken light fixtures.

"Whoa!" said Pasquale. "I hope Kermit has insurance."

News reporters had already moved in on the scene and were shoving cameras in our faces.

CAN YOU TELL US WHAT HAPPENED?

DID YOU WITNESS THE DESTRUCTION?

ARE ALL THE MEMBERS OF M.E.S.S. SAFE?

AREN'T YOU THAT MUPPET KID?

WHAT'S NINE PLUS NINE DIVIDED BY TWO?

"I'm sorry," I said, pushing the cameras away. "No comment. I have to find my friends."

As we searched the rubble, Kermit and Scooter walked out covered in dust but still intact. More and more Muppets crawled out behind them. Scooter pulled out a clipboard and started calling out names to make sure everyone was accounted for.

I ran over to Kermit. "Kermit! You're okay!"

"Yep," he said, dusting off his flippers. "Aside from a little frog in my throat, I feel fine. That was a little amphibian humor for you."

I looked around frantically, but couldn't find my boss. "Where's Gonzo?" I cried.

The news reporters spotted Kermit and zoomed in for an interview. He was hit with a barrage of questions.

"Relax, people! Everyone is safe and uninjured!" Kermit announced to the cameras.

"But, Mr. Kermit," asked a reporter, "how do you respond to reports that this was caused by Animal, rock drummer for The Electric Mayhem Band, grown to an enormous size?"

"I'd say you were just trying to drum up a good story!"

"What about that humongous footprint in the ground over there?" asked another reporter.

But the reporters just wouldn't quit. "What about these pictures of Animal doing a radical drum solo using two telephone poles and the Block City Sports Dome?"

Kermit looked flummoxed. "Uh...no comment. But for your information, Animal is just fine. Why, here he comes now."

One last question from the media really seemed to rattle Kermit. "Mr. the Frog, isn't it true that this incident, along with all the other odd occurrences, including the recent ground tremors, are linked to Mr. Blickensderfer's transformation and could quite possibly signal the end of the world?"

Kermit looked miffed. "That's preposterous. Who is your source on that?"

"A great journalist never reveals his source," said the reporter, "but it rhymes with *Lobo*."

"It seems like there's something Kermit isn't telling us," I whispered to Pasquale. "He looks jumpy, and his palms are clammy."

"He *is* a frog," Pasquale pointed out.

But I knew it was something more. I could see a look of concern on Kermit's face.

Suddenly, a huge chunk of debris fell over with a tremendous *crash* and a disheveled Miss Piggy came crawling out, huffing and puffing.

"Call it a day?" Piggy huffed.

Kermit ran over to her. "Aw, Piggy! I hadn't noticed you were missing, but I'm so happy you made it out unscathed."

"Hadn't *noticed*? *Unscathed*?" roared Piggy. "I'll show you unscathed! Hiiiiiii-yaaaaaaa!"

Scooter helped clear away the rest of the media and answer any questions the cops had. As soon as the reporters had gone, he turned to me and Pasquale and said, "Whew! That was close."

"What do you mean?" I asked.

"The situation has gotten grim," he warned. "We have to act soon."

I THINK IT'S TIME WE HAD ANOTHER MEETING AT OUR SECRET GOVERNMENT HEADQUARTERS.

SOUNDS GOOD. MAYBE WE SHOULD CALL AHEAD TO ORDER CHEESY BREAD.

TOP SECRET

The mood was serious as we all sat

around the conference table at Pepperoni Planet. Well, once we got Statler and Waldorf away from the foosball table, at least.

AS A YOUNG LAD, I USED TO IMPRESS ALL THE LADIES WITH MY FOOSBALL-PLAYING PROWESS!

WAS THAT BEFORE OR AFTER YOU CAME OVER ON THE *MAYFLOWER*? HA HA!

Kermit stood up and addressed the room. "Guys, I feel just rotten about what happened today. Not only did the theater get damaged and some of you got scuffed up, but I had to fib to the media."

"What did you lie about?" asked Pasquale.

"You told them green is your natural collar color, didn't you?" said Rizzo.

"No." Kermit sighed. "It was worse than that. I lied about Animal destroying the theater."

"So he really did grow to an enormous size and use the Sports Dome as a drum set?" I asked.

"Luckily, the effect on Animal was only temporary," said Dr. Honeydew.

As I examined the jar of Insta-Grow Pills, I realized this was another example of my theory coming true. "You do realize," I pointed out, "that Animal ate some of these pills in *The Muppet Movie*? These were just supposed to be make-believe."

"That's why we are here," said Kermit. "At first it was kinda kooky and fun to mix up reality and fantasy. But now it has gotten dangerous. We can't have giant Animals rampaging through the city."

"Or an army of Beakers tormenting their employer just because he once subjected them to dangerous experiments involving fire ants and corn syrup," added Dr. Honeydew.

I put one of the Insta-Grow Pills in my pocket. I figured it might come in handy next time I was trying out for the wrestling team.

Kermit looked very serious. "I'm afraid we have to act now. We must send Danvers through Wormhole N-1 in the next few days."

"There is another way," said Dr. Honeydew. "But we will have to look to the private sector."

I pulled Pasquale aside. "Dude, see how crazy things are getting? The *Swinetrek* was a fictional spaceship in a Muppet skit called 'Pigs in Space.' It's not even real."

"I don't care if it's real or not," Pasquale said, beaming. "We're going to outer space! I wonder what I should pack? You think I should take three pairs of underwear or four?"

Kermit stopped Pasquale in his tracks. "Pasquale, I'm afraid that only Danvers and the crew of the *Swinetrek* will be going on this mission. It's too dangerous for anyone else to go."

Pasquale's face fell. He looked crushed. "But it's my dream to travel to space like my astronaut heroes," he moaned. "How else will I be able to trace the origins of the big bang theory?"

"Have you tried reruns?" said Rizzo.

I'M SORRY, KIDDO. BUT I AM OBLIGATED TO MAKE SURE ONLY PROFESSIONAL SPACE TRAVELERS WITH UNPARALLELED TRAINING AND KNOWLEDGE OF ASTROPHYSICS ARE ON BOARD. WELL, AND DANVERS.

HMMM, IT SAYS HERE THAT SINCE WE LAST TRAVELED TO SPACE, PLUTO IS NO LONGER CONSIDERED A PLANET.

BUT OF COURSE. I KNEW HE WAS A DOG ALL ALONG. NOW, WHAT THE HECK IS GOOFY?

I could tell that Pasquale was really bummed, but Kermit promised him a top-notch position at mission control to make him feel better. Dr. Honeydew and Strangepork agreed that we could only allow three days for training and preparation. Three days! That seemed like a crazy-short amount of time to organize an interstellar voyage. But I knew something even more daunting lay ahead—getting permission from my parents.

IS IT TOO LATE TO GET SOME OF THAT CHEESY BREAD?

The Muppet Theater sent out a special convoy of folks the next morning to help convince Sam Eagle to allow me to miss some school so I could save the world, and also to let us use his school gym facilities for the rigorous training. I knew it would be a tough sell. We sat him down at his desk and explained everything in great detail.

Scooter stepped in and went through the entire story and our planet-saving plan in English. When he finished, Sam thought it over for a while.

"So what you want me to do is authorize the launching of one of my students into deep space?" Sam pondered. "Couldn't we send Phips Terlington instead? That child is working my last nerve."

AND IF I LET ONE KID HAVE HIS ATOMS REARRANGED AFTER BEING HURLED THROUGH A RADIOACTIVE WORMHOLE IN THE COLD VACUUM OF SPACE, THEN ALL THE KIDS WILL WANT TO DO IT.

But I used some reverse psychiatry on him. "Just think, Sam Eagle. If you say yes, when all is said and done, you will forever be known as the school principal who saved the planet or, better yet, the principal who saved America! It'll be a real feather in your cap."

"Hmmm," said Sam. "As a bald eagle, I could use another feather in my cap. In case you haven't noticed, I suffer from male pattern molting."

Kermit went in for the kill. "Sam Eagle—American

hero! What great PR for Eagle Talon Academy! I bet they'll name a new annex of the school after you."

"A new annex," Sam repeated, pondering the idea. "I have always wanted to add the Sam Eagle Right Wing."

OH, HECK! WHY NOT? EAGLE TALON ACADEMY HAS ALWAYS BEEN KNOWN FOR ITS PATRIOTISM AND BRAVERY. THAT IS WHY OUR SCHOOL MASCOT IS THE AMERICAN BALD PYGMY SHREW. I SAY LET'S GO FOR IT!

OH, GOOD!

GO SHREWS!

"I do have one stipulation," added Sam. "In case there is anyone left in this town who doesn't know, Danvers's grades are appalling. If he does go to space, he must continue to receive daily lessons in math and science while aboard the *Swinetrek*."

AS MY GREAT-GRANDFATHER USED TO SAY, "LEARNING MUST NEVER BE IMPEDED BY INTERGALACTIC TRAVEL TO ALIEN WORMHOLES."

NEVER FEAR. HOWIE 5000 WILL BE ON BOARD AS A MATH TUTOR. DANVERS WILL SPEND TWO HOURS DAILY STUDYING THE WONDERS OF MATHEMATICS AND SCIENCE.

GEE, THAT'S JUST SWELL.

MATH IS FUN! HA! HA!

At lunch that day, I kinda just wanted to be alone because too much stuff was going through my head. I was nervous about going to space, nervous about the weird changes and tremors gripping the planet, and nervous about having to pass math. Plus, Hockney wasn't known for his electrifying lunchroom conversation.

I took the lunch my mom had bagged for me to the courtyard outside Eagle Talon Academy and plopped down on a bench. As I removed the foil-wrapped lump from my brown bag and tore it open, my heart sank; one of Mom's leftover meat-loaf sandwiches was staring back at me.

Then it talked to me.

WHAT'S UP, HOMESLICE?

I couldn't believe it! Mom's meat loaf was capable of a lot of things—frightening small children, causing irreversible intestinal damage, serving as an emergency brick substitute—but…talking?!

"Ya mind putting me down, kid?" said the meat loaf. "If I'm late for class, I'm gonna be in a real *pickle!*"

"Are you a-a student?" I stuttered back. "A Muppet sandwich?"

"No. No. I'm just a sub! Get it? A *sub*! Ha!"

WAIT A SEC! YOU'RE A SUBSTITUTE TEACHER?

YEAH. THE PAY DOESN'T REALLY CUT THE *MUSTARD*, BUT I'VE GOT ENOUGH *BREAD* TO AFFORD A DECENT SPREAD. AND I *RELISH* THE CHALLENGE! HEY-OOOOH! GOTTA GO!

My snarky sandwich took off toward class. (Just in case anyone ever asks you how meat-loaf sandwiches get around, they hop and slide, kinda like any other sandwich.)

The world really was spinning out of control. I was already on edge over my talking lunch when, suddenly, the Earth started to tremble again, only this time it was more violent. I leaned down and put my hand to the ground. It rolled and fluctuated almost like it was a fluid, except it still felt hard on top, a lot like Swedish Chef's butterscotch pudding.

"Whoa," I said to myself. "Talking sandwiches. Liquefied earth. Things are getting worse."

That's when the tree across the courtyard caught my attention. It looked a little strange. The leaves weren't blowing in the breeze like usual. I slowly approached it and looked around the trunk only to discover that the tree was just a one-dimensional backdrop, like the set for a Muppet skit.

Then a warbly, awful voice drifted across the courtyard. It was a horrible song of some sort, and it was coming from the trash can. *First my sandwich, and now the garbage cans are coming to life,* I thought as I inched toward the crooning can. *What other horrors lie in store for me?*

Suddenly, a skeletal beast with flaming red hair popped out!

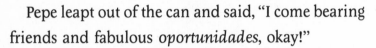

Pepe leapt out of the can and said, "I come bearing friends and fabulous *oportunidades*, okay!"

"Friends?" I said.

Pepe pointed over to the shrubs near the trash can. "I bring my entourage, okay."

Some familiar faces came crawling out of the foliage.

It was Kip, Danny, and Cody, my former class-mates from Coldrain. We had all teamed up a while back to form the boy-band supergroup M.E.S.S., and to our total shock, our song, "Girl, Don't Be Rash," an ode to poison ivy and young love, had become a smash hit. It was so popular we were hired to be the official band of Ivy League Poison Ivy Itch Crème, and we even made a summer-camp TV movie. But we hadn't recorded anything since.

"What the heck are you guys doing?" I yelled. "You can't be here! Aren't you supposed to be in class?"

"Se calmer mon ami!" snapped Danny.

"Don't worry, yo," said Kip. "We all called in sick to school today."

"You mean you're playing hooky?"

"Naw, dude. We were just feeling discombobulated." Kip grinned. "It wasn't our idea, yo."

The shrubs rustled, and all of a sudden Pasquale stepped out, covered in leaves.

"Pasquale?" I said. "I can't believe you would play hooky from Coldrain and show up here! You could get them all expelled."

Pasquale looked down at his sneakers, a little ashamed.

"Don't be hatin' on your best bud, yo," said Kip. "We're here because it's an emergency! The end is near!"

I perked up a bit. "You mean you've noticed that the tremors and oddities have increased today, too? I thought maybe it was just me."

"No, no, dude!" cried Kip. "I'm talking about something much more important—my band, yo! We're in trouble! If we don't get a hit soon, you can just go ahead and book us on *Celebrity Has-Been Dance Squad*!"

Long before we had all teamed up to form M.E.S.S., Kip had his own boy band called Emo Shun. They used to be the hottest band in school, but things hadn't been going so well since they started experimenting with other musical styles.

Kip grabbed me by my shoulders. "We're doomed, dawg! Our heavy metal album just isn't meeting our sales forecast. Plus, we upset the Mother Hens of America!"

The album was not one of their best efforts, I have to admit, but I was confused. "What does this have to do with skipping school and sneaking into Eagle Talon?"

"We had to catch you before you took off on the *Swinetrek*," said Kip. "I got this fly idea, yo. We should team up again for another M.E.S.S. single. Only this time, we sing about planets instead of poison ivy, and we broadcast it from outer space."

I was completely irked that Kip knew about the secret mission. I turned and gave Pasquale a look that would make Miss Piggy tremble. "And *how* did you find out about my space-travel plans?"

Pasquale looked up from his feet. "It was my fault. Sofi and I were talking about Pepperoni Planet, and I blabbed about the meeting we had there. Then she blabbed to Kip….Hey, wait a minute. What was she doing hanging out with you, Kip?"

"Uh, that's not important right now, yo," said Kip. "What is important is this amazing opportunity. The chance to sing our message of love to all the girls across the universe. I've already written the song. It's called 'Step to My Neptune.'"

Pepe added, "And I, as your publicizer, will work with Rizzo to create a website so we can stream the first music video from another galaxy and de people can pay us money to log on, okay."

It was a great idea—the thought of crooning to all the ladies from light-years away was awesome—but I had to shoot it down. "Sorry, dudes. But this is about saving the planet, not impressing girls and selling records. I don't know if you noticed, but the weird phenomena have really kicked it up a notch. I mean, have you ever had your sandwich run off before you could eat it?"

"I had some runny eggs for breakfast, yo," said Kip.

"I'm sorry, guys," I said. "I hate to rain on your parade, but you have to drop this idea. And another thing—this mission is totally top secret! You can't tell anyone else, okay?"

"I respect your decision, yo." Kip sighed. "We won't tell anyone else. I guess we should make sure Sofi and her friends don't spread it around, too. Oh, and I should probably delete it from my blog."

Pasquale looked like a deflated, depressed balloon as they all turned and headed off back into the shrubs.

After lunch, Sam Eagle cleared out

the gymnasium for us and had Miss Piggy, Link, and Dr. Strangepork brought in through the secret rear entrance.

> OH, THIS IS SO EXCITING! SNEAKING IN THROUGH THE BACK. IT REMINDS *MOI* OF A TIME BEFORE MY MOVIE CAREER, WHEN I GAVE SOLD-OUT LIVE PERFORMANCES.

> I'M NOT SURE ZAT LIVESTOCK SHOWS COUNT AS PERFORMANCES. HEE! HEE! HEE!

> GOOD ONE, DOC!

After Piggy dished out two prime karate chops, we all met in the center of the gym with Sam. We had the whole joint to ourselves.

"Wow!" I said. "How did you get all the kids to clear out of here?"

"Easy," answered Sam. "I just announced that I would soon be performing my one-bird show, *Benjamin Franklin: Ben There, Done That*, followed by a pop quiz."

"Thank you, Sam Eagle. I shall take it from here," said Dr. Strangepork. Sam left, and the pig continued. "The reason ve are here is to prepare your bodies for the unforgiving harshness of space travel. To do this, ve have brought in a special guest trainer. Danvers, you should recognize him."

Suddenly, I got a lump of pure terror in my throat as a dark shadow came over us.

"Please velcome Coach Kraft, on loan from Cold-rain Middle School," said Strangepork. "Ve thought you might appreciate seeing a familiar face, Mr. Blickensderfer."

"Thanks," I whimpered. "I usually see that face in my nightmares."

Coach Kraft slapped his hands and bellowed, "I want your undivided attention, scuzzbuckets! First things first—I am not here to be your friend! I'm also not here to be your mommy or your nanny or your pappy or your coffee barista or your accountant—although if you need your taxes done at a reasonable rate, my cousin on the South Side is your man. I'll give you his number after—"

"Ahem!" coughed Dr. Strangepork. "Excuse me, Coach. Since I am in flawless, tip-top physical condition, I shall just have a seat over zere on the bleachers und sip on my cranberry juice pouch."

Piggy flipped her hair back dramatically and said, "Oh, Coach? Surely you won't make *moi* strain herself. After all, *moi* is wearing high heels, which are totally unfit for exercise."

"High-heeled shoes?" roared Coach. "Gimme those!"

He plucked the pumps right off Piggy's feet.

What followed was the most exhausting workout I've ever had. Forget the *Navy Seal Breakneck Boot Camp* workout video or the Groovin' Grannies Aerobics Plan—Coach Kraft's astronaut training was a killer!

Coach Kraft's Three-day Astronaut "CRUNCH" course

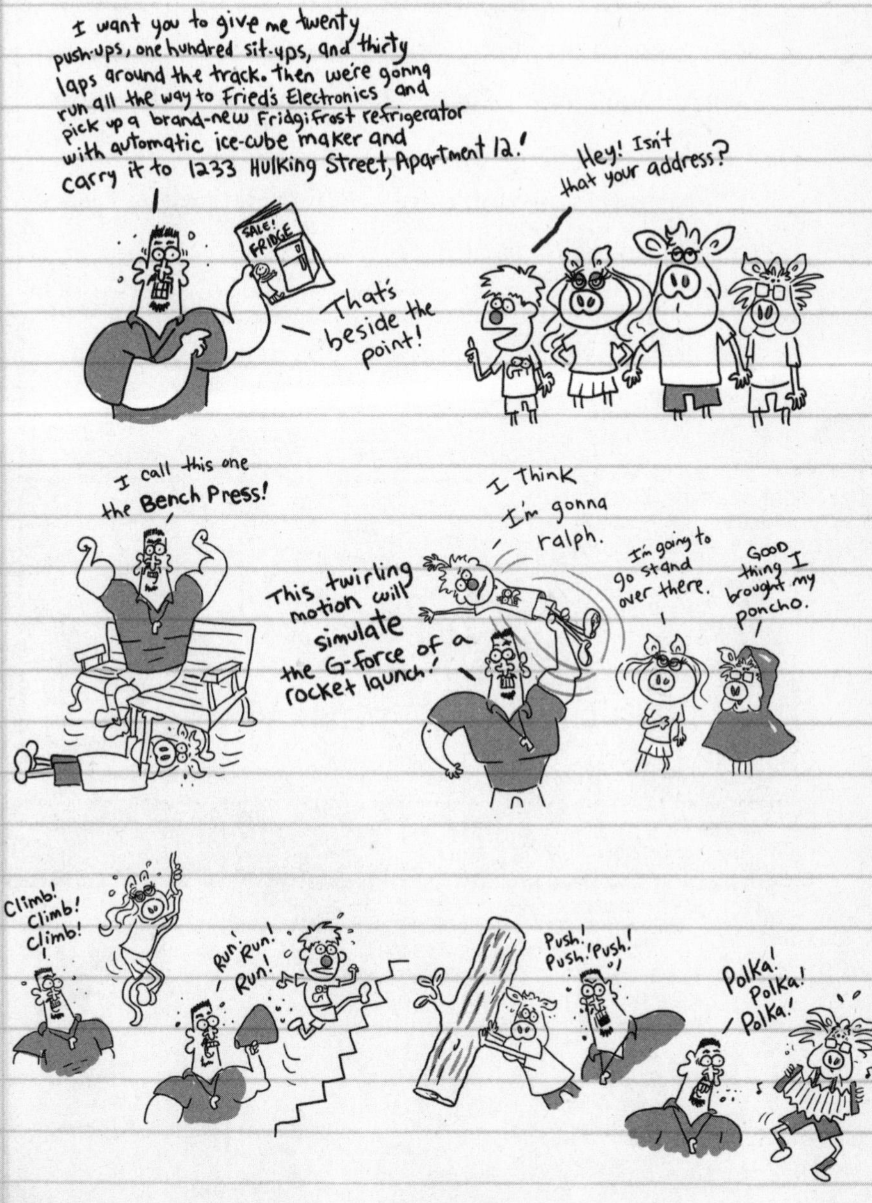

The running and jumping and climbing and wrestling were so intense that at the end we collapsed in a sweaty, heaving heap.

"Uuuugh!" cried Piggy. "This is so undignified for a pig! I feel terrible!"

"I'm sure you don't feel half as terrible as you look," Link said, panting.

"If I had any strength left," Piggy said, fuming, "I'd come over there and use your snout as a boot scraper!"

Walking home that afternoon, it was a chore just lifting my legs for even one step after the brutal training Coach Kraft had inflicted on us. Plus, the weird earthquakes were getting more and more frequent. Some folks were running around screaming about the end of the world. Newspapers featured noted scientists making dire predictions. And the freakiest thing of all: On every corner, behind every tree, on every park bench were the Beakers. There were Beakers everywhere! Watching. Waiting. Meeping.

The *meeps* drowned out all other sounds, getting louder and louder, like cicadas on a hot summer day. I picked up my pace. Soon I was sprinting back to my apartment. I got to the front door and bolted inside, locking it behind me. I was home. I was safe...

Or was I?

Curtis immediately ran up my leg and hugged my neck, trembling.

"What's the matter, Curtis?" I said, petting him on the back. He pointed toward the kitchen and squeaked.

I could see my mom in the kitchen. Strange, peppy music was playing, and it looked like she was dancing. Suddenly I remembered the meat loaf that had come to life earlier in the day. I rushed to the kitchen to warn her.

"Hey, Mom! Stay away from the meat loaf in the fridge! It's alive and snarky!"

Mom gave me a strange look. "I know it's alive, Danvers. We've been chatting for the last hour. He's very funny."

I pulled my mom into the living room and whimpered. "Mom! Something weird is happening to the world, and that wisecracking meat loaf is just the beginning. The Earth is in deep—"

A loud snoring sound interrupted my rant. I looked around the living room, confused. "What's making that noise?"

I grabbed my mom by the arm. "Okay, Mom, this is getting crazy. The meat loaf and the couch are alive, and Dad just made a joke. Can't you see that things are out of whack?"

"I don't know what you're talking about, Danvers," my mom said robotically as she walked over and clicked on the television. "Let's watch some TV."

Channel Seven featured a news guy who was going nuts.

SCIENTISTS ARE NOW SAYING THAT THE STRANGE OCCURRENCES AND EARTHQUAKES MAY SIGNAL THE IMPENDING END OF THE WORLD! RUMOR HAS IT THAT YOUNG DANVERS BLICKENSDERFER, THE BOY WHO BECAME A MUPPET, IS LAUNCHING INTO SPACE TOMORROW ON A SECRET MISSION TO PREVENT OUR ANNIHILATION.

Darn that Bobo and his big mouth, I thought, *Now the media is going to be all over us.*

"Is there something you need to tell us, Danvers?" asked my mom, looking worried. "I hope what he said is not true, about you going to space and all. I thought that permission slip we signed was for a trip to Hollywood."

"Mom," I pleaded. "Okay! I know I should have been honest with you about that, but please, you have to understand, if I don't get to the Wormhole N-1 and reverse the Muppetmorphosis, the whole planet could blow up!"

Mom didn't look convinced. "Sweetie, I just can't approve of you gallivanting across the universe. You're only in sixth grade."

All of a sudden we heard a huge *CHOMP!* and the blaring TV went silent.

Mom looked back at me. "Maybe things *are* getting a little unstable."

A loud banging on the front door made us all jump. I ran to the door and opened it to find a panicked Kermit and Dr. Teeth.

"Thank goodness you're here!" cried Kermit. "The situation has obviously escalated. Now that the press is onto us, we've decided to launch tonight!"

I nearly choked. "Tonight?"

"Otherwise the media will find our secret launch site and it'll be a madhouse! Even madder than this house. I don't know if you noticed, but the couch is eating your dad."

After we helped pluck Dad from the jaws of our sofa, I hugged my parents tight. "I gotta do this, guys," I cried.

"Well, at least be careful out there," said my dad.

"And don't go too fast in that spaceship," added Mom. "Mach 2 at the fastest."

"And you've gotta stay here, too, you little devil," I said to Curtis.

"You'd better go say good-bye to your sister, too," my mom said with a sigh.

"Do I have to?" I groaned. "Can't I just send her a postcard from the moons of Jupiter or something?"

My parents just gave me a cold stare. "All right! I'll do it," I said.

But it wasn't meant to be. Just then a huge, rolling, rocking quake rumbled through the apartment! Plaster fell from the ceiling, the walls cracked, and books flew off their shelves.

"Go on, son!" yelled my dad. "We'll be okay."

As we rushed out the door, Kermit said, "The bus is waiting to take us to the top secret launch location!"

I looked back at my tiny apartment, hoping that this wouldn't be the last time I saw it.

The Electric Mayhem Bus sped through the countryside, taking blind turns at the speed of a…well, the speed of a worn-out, rusty bus. It was packed to the brim with Muppets, who were all jazzed to watch the launch. I was a nervous wreck, and I kept glancing out the windows for any signs of reporters tailing us.

"The rest of the *Swinetrek* crew members are already at the launch site," said Kermit.

"What about Pasquale?" I asked.

"He's probably at mission control, helping Dr. Honeydew."

Looking around the bus, I couldn't help but notice several missing faces. No Animal, Gonzo, Fozzie, Pepe, or Rizzo. I shrugged and figured they were already at the site.

Rowlf could tell I was nervous, so he tried to keep the mood light by telling a joke. Soon, everyone was in on the action.

WOW! TEETH, I THINK YOU JUST SET A NEW LONG-DISTANCE RECORD!

BROKE THE LAWS OF PHYSICS, TOO, BUT IT SURE MADE FOR AN EXCITING ACTION SCENE.

Beakers avoided, we sped down the road and crested a big hill, where we came upon a magnificent sight—standing in the middle of a huge pasture was the mighty *Swinetrek*. Or, I should say, wallowed the mighty *Swinetrek*.

The *Swinetrek* was sitting on a ginormous mud-covered trough that stretched for hundreds of yards and sloped upward like a ramp. There were guys in yellow safety suits hosing the ramp down with gallons of mud.

My flip-top mouth fell open. "It's so huge! And covered in mud. That thing is filthy!"

"Looks like we might need to *scrub* the launch!" snarked Rowlf, brandishing a soapy sponge.

"Noooooooo!" said a voice with a familiar accent. It was Dr. Strangepork, pulling up in a moon buggy with Miss Piggy and Link Hogthrob, all of them decked out in some seriously killer metallic space duds. "That mud is essential to the *Svinetrek*'s launch!"

ZE MUD IS A SPECIAL FORMULA CREATED BY MYSELF UND MANUFACTURED BY THE BRILLIANT MINDS OF **SSSPTSSST!**

WATCH THE HAIR, DOC! I JUST HAD IT SHELLACKED WITH HAIR SPRAY.

Dr. Strangepork pulled out a canister and poured some of the mud in his hand. "It is a special compound. When ve apply high-voltage electricity, the mud is ionized, creating nine million pigawatts of energy that will send the *Svinetrek* hurtling up the blast-trough und into the stratosphere!"

IT ALSO MAKES A GREAT FACIAL MASK. IT REALLY OPENS UP MY PORES AND MINIMIZES THE FINE LINES AROUND MY SNOUT.

OH, BROTHER!

Another pulsating rumble rippled through the earth, and the mud sloshed and gurgled around the *Swinetrek.*

"Oooh!" cried Dr. Strangepork. "Zat vas a big one! Ve've got to hurry! The quakes are getting more violent!"

"And I'm...I'm feeling kind of str-str-straaange," Kermit moaned, looking a little woozy. Then he pulled out his *Muppet Treasure Island* captain's hat and plopped it on his noggin.

AYE! AYE! AND WE MUST ALSO BEWARE OF LONG JOHN SILVER! MY FIRST MATE UP IN THE CROW'S NEST REPORTS THAT THE LILY-LIVERED SCOUNDREL APPROACHES ON THE PORT BOW!

OH, NO! SNAP OUT OF IT, KERMIT! STAY WITH US!

STEP ASIDE, KID. I'VE GOT JUST THE THING TO JOLT HIM BACK TO HIS SENSES. HIIIIIII-YAAAAAAA!

Piggy gave Kermit one heck of a chop, and he went sailing into the mud. Piggy ran over to him to help him back up. "Oh, Kermieeeeee! Piggy is so sorry she had to do that, but it was the only way to bring you out of your delusions."

Kermit took off his hat and shook his head. "It's okay, Piggy. At least you had a good reason that time. Sorry I slipped back into swashbuckling mode again. Boy! We better get you guys on that ship! Come on!"

"But I need to stop by mission control and tell Pasquale good-bye!" I said. "This might be the last time I get to see him."

"I'm sorry, Danvers," said Kermit, "but there's just no time! We've gotta get you on board!"

I knew he was right, but it was a bummer. "I looked up at the mission control window at the top of a big red barn by the launch site, gave a wave, then looked to the *Swinetrek*.

"Let's do this!" I shouted.

Kermit and I hopped in the buggy with the crew, and we sped off toward the ship.

F

"reeze-dried astronaut ice cream."

"Check!"

"Personal stun gun laser blaster."

"Check!"

"Transfiguration receptor mini-console."

"Check!"

Link and Dr. Strangepork were running through their preflight checklist as Kermit helped me and Piggy buckle in.

"Extra toothbrush."

"Check!"

MR. SNUGGYBEAR AND COMFY BLANKIE SO CAPTAIN HOGTHROB CAN GO NAPPY TIME.

CHECK!

The flight deck of the ship had more bleepy lights and shiny gadgets than ten Pepperoni Planet Pizza Parlor arcades put together. There was a big screen behind us. On it was Dr. Honeydew, dressed in dark shades, wearing a fedora, fake mustache, and beard.

"Dr. Honeydew, why are you in disguise?" I asked over the intercom.

I HAD TO GO INCOGNITO TO GET AWAY FROM ALL THOSE BEAKERS. THERE'S JUST WAY TOO MUCH OF HIM TO GO AROUND, I'M AFRAID. FOR SOME REASON HE SEEMS TO BE DISGRUNTLED ABOUT THE TIME I GENETICALLY CROSSED HIM WITH A PRAYING MANTIS.

"Can you put Pasquale on?" I asked the doc. "I wanna tell him adios."

"I'm afraid Pasquale isn't here," said Dr. Honeydew. "We tried to locate him, but to no avail. This launch was rather last-minute."

I was bummed. Not only was I not going to be able to say good-bye, but Pasquale was going to miss out on the launch.

"I've bolted the door to the control room," Dr. Honeydew continued. "No one can get in unless they use the secret knock."

"Oh, boy!" said Kermit. "That could take a while. I better get off this ship and rush over there. Good luck, you guys!"

Piggy grabbed Kermit for a dramatic good-bye. "Oh, Kermie!"

AU REVOIR, MY LITTLE GREEN AMOUR. ISN'T THERE ANYTHING VOUS WOULD LIKE TO TELL MOI BEFORE I'M OFF ON WHAT COULD BE MY FINAL, DANGEROUS MISSION ACROSS THE VAST, UNFORGIVING VOID OF OUTER SPACE?

UH... HAVE A NICE TRIP?

"Have a nice trip?" growled Piggy. She dropped Kermit like a sack of sawdust and stormed off.

"Sheesh! What did I say?" cried Kermit.

"It's probably what you didn't say," I suggested.

"You take off in five minutes," advised Dr. Honeydew. "I will control the launch from here on the ground, then Captain Hogthrob can take over once you've cleared the Earth's atmosphere."

"No need for that!" said Dr. Strangepork, wheeling in the HOWIE 5000. "HOWIE 5000 is virelessly hooked into the ship's computer. He can control the launch und the navigation all automatically. The captain really doesn't even have to do anything."

"What else is new?" said Piggy.

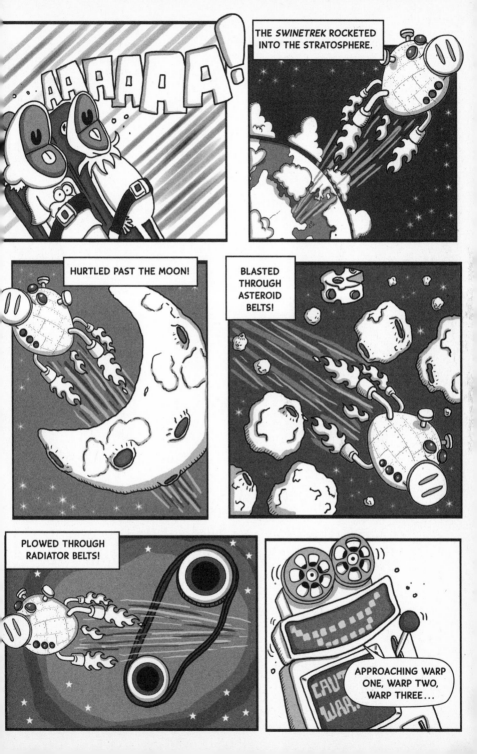

"Hey, HOWIE!" yelled Piggy. "I think you can slow down now! This pig is falling apart on us."

"Negative," HOWIE replied.

"Don't vorry. The *Svinetrek* is a sturdy ship," Dr. Strangepork assured her.

"I was talking about him," said Piggy, pointing at Link.

"HOWIE, you need to slow us down!" Kermit cried.

"Negative," the robot repeated, ignoring us.

I unstrapped my seat belt and crawled over to Kermit. "Maybe we should unplug HOWIE 5000 from the ship's computers," I suggested.

"It's no use," said Kermit. "He's controlling the ship with Wi-Fi!"

"I've got a better idea!" bellowed Piggy, unleashing a karate chop on the renegade computer.

HOWIE jolted Miss Piggy with an electric shock so strong, the force of it sent her sailing clear across the bridge.

"Owww!" she groaned as Kermit and Link helped her up off the floor.

"My apologies, excitable porcine creature," said HOWIE. "My circuits are equipped with an automatic defense mechanism. Anyone who tries to interfere with my control of the ship will receive five thousand volts of electricity, no quarter required."

ON THE POSITIVE SIDE— YOUR NEW HAIRDO LOOKS ELECTRIFYING.

HMMMMMMPH!

I tried to reason with the computer. "Look, Mr. 5000, would you mind just slowing down a little? Just to put everyone's minds at ease?"

HOWIE looked at me, then relented. "Okay. Only because you, the greatest boy-band lead singer in the universe—I mean world!—asked me to."

"Uh…that's great, HOWIE," I said, a little weirded out. "Then let's just make sure we get to the wormhole safely. You wouldn't want to harm your favorite performer."

The ship finally slowed down, and we all let out a deep breath.

"Whew!" I said.

Dr. Strangepork checked the mapping computer for our coordinates. "Hmmm…it seems ve are already ten million miles from Earth, according to our GPS. That's the Global Pork Satellite."

A staticky voice blared out over the speakers. "Come in, *Swinetrek*! SS *Swinetrek*, come in, over!"

It was Dr. Honeydew! His image popped up onto the video screen, but it was fuzzy and glitchy.

Piggy spoke into the intercom. "This is the SS *Swinetrek*. Whaddaya want?"

Dr. Honeydew seemed exasperated. "Thank goodness! We thought we had lost you after that premature launch!"

"We thought so, too!" Piggy huffed. "Thanks a lot for hooking us up with this whackjob of a computer!"

"Is everyone on board okay?" asked Honeydew.

"Yes, we're all right!" said Kermit. "How are things on Earth?"

"Well, the housing market is still touch-and-go, and the polar ice caps are shrinking, but there is hope on the jobs front...."

"No, no! I mean are the tremors and weird phenomena getting any worse?"

"Oh," said Dr. Honeydew. "Yes, I'm afraid so, Kermit. That's what I need to talk to you about. I have Danvers's parents with me, and they have an important message for their son about what's happening!"

I jumped up. "My parents?"

"Put 'em on, Doc!" said Kermit.

MOM! DAD!

DANVERS! THERE'S SOMETHING WE HAVE TO TELL YOU ABOUT CHLOE! SHE IS—

Suddenly, with a jagged flash, the screen went blank!

"Come in, mission control!" said Piggy. "I repeat, come in, mission control! Yoo-hoo?"

"My sister is what?" I cried. "Piggy! What happened to the image?"

Piggy adjusted her intercom controls and tapped on her headset. "I lost 'em, kid."

"Oh, darn," said HOWIE 5000. "We must have traveled too far out of range. Guess we'll never know."

I didn't know what to think. Had the world just blown up? Were we just disconnected? Had the *Swinetrek*'s mobile plan just run out of minutes? And what did my folks want to tell me about Chloe? Was she okay?

I couldn't help but feel that HOWIE had something to do with losing the signal.

"Well, then," HOWIE said. "Maintain course. I'm going to the little computer room to powder my CPU."

HOWIE rolled out through the sliding door, and we all huddled in the middle of the bridge.

"This HOWIE character is a couple of heating

elements short of a toaster oven," said Kermit. "I'm afraid he might jeopardize our mission."

"Yeah, usually computers with creepy voices that run spaceships are so reliable und friendly," said Strangepork.

"Well, we better just humor him until we can find a way to shut him down," I whispered. "Until then, we should—"

I stopped cold. Something was bulging in my shirt, moving across my chest.

"What is that?" screamed Piggy.

"I don't know!" I cried as the bulge moved up toward my neck.

"What is it, boy?" I asked. "Something's really got Curtis upset."

Link was not happy. "No one told me there were going to be filthy animals on this flight!"

"I vould like to point out zat you are a pig who likes mud," said Dr. Strangepork. "So, chill out."

"The mud is a beauty treatment," muttered Link.

"I can't believe it," I said, scratching Curtis under the chin. "My own rat, a stowaway. If this were a pirate ship, you'd have to walk the plank for this."

"Let's drop the pirate talk in front of Kermie," Piggy whispered in my ear.

"Good call, Piggy," I said.

It was actually kind of nice to have Curtis on board. I had been missing him terribly already. But Curtis wasn't there to cuddle with me. He had a serious look in his beady little eyes. He squeaked and tugged at my shirt.

"Curtis wants us to follow him into the hall," I said. "He must have caught a whiff of something out there."

Dr. Strangepork pulled out a buzzing contraption and said, "Perhaps he has picked up on the scent of another stowaway. My sensors have detected multiple uninvited guests near the dining quarters."

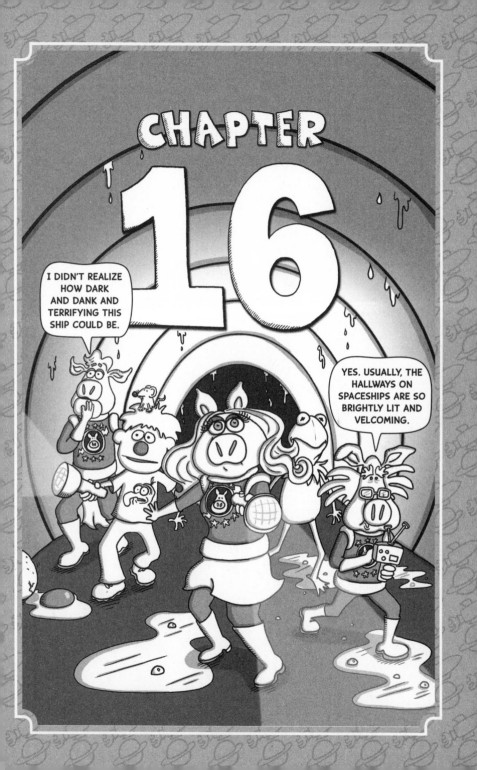

The corridors of the *Swinetrek* were dark and dripping with condensation. Piggy led the way as we slowly slunk through the halls, our stun pistols at the ready.

All was silent except for the knocking of Link Hogthrob's knees and the beeping of Dr. Strangepork's sensor. As we rounded a corner, his device started to ping louder and louder. Curtis clutched my neck tight.

"My sensors indicate that ve are dealing vith either multiple intruders or one morbidly obese circus elephant!" said Dr. Strangepork.

The meter really started going crazy as soon as we reached the broom closet.

I pressed a button next to the door, and it slid open. Out fell three stow-aways!

As the intruders stood up and dust-ed themselves off, Link screamed and hid his eyes with his hands. But I wasn't so scared. Standing before us were the members of Emo Shun: Kip, Cody, and Danny!

"What are you guys doing here?" I yelled. "You about gave us a heart attack!"

"Uh," said Kip, "we're not actually here, yo. We're just holograms. Our real bodies are a million miles away on Earth, dude."

IF YOU'RE A HOLOGRAM, THEN YOU SHOULDN'T FEEL IT WHEN I KICK YOU.

OW, YO! YOU DON'T HAVE TO GET HOSTILE. OKAY, SO WE HID ON BOARD BECAUSE WE THOUGHT WE COULD TALK YOU INTO DOING THAT MUSIC-VIDEO-FROM-SPACE THING. IT'S JUST TOO GOOD AN OPPORTUNITY TO PASS UP, YO.

"Music video?" said Kermit.

"Yeah." Kip perked up. "Imagine it! Our smoldering love jams pumped into every home in the galaxy from the farthest regions of outer space, yo. It'll be epic!"

"I told these guys I wasn't interested," I assured Kermit. "But they hid on board anyway."

Kermit was not happy. "Pepe! Rizzo! This is a dangerous mission."

"Yeah," added Piggy, "how are we going to explain to these kids' parents that their sons are in another solar system when they're supposed to be at home, in bed?"

"Maybe you can tell them they were eaten by rabid mongooses, okay," said Pepe.

Rizzo grabbed Kermit by the arm. "Just think of it, Kermit! The first boy band in space! Imagine the headlines! The fame! The *ka-ching*!"

"There will be no headlines, fame, or *ka-chinging*, because there will be no music video from space," Kermit said. "Sorry, guys."

"Ohhh, boy." Pepe sighed. "Then I guess we won't need the safety officer, either, okay."

"What safety officer?" I asked. That's when Pasquale came lumbering out of the closet as well, looking very embarrassed. I couldn't believe my eyes.

"Hey," he said with a sigh.

"Pasquale!" I roared. "How could you? I expect this of Kip, but you?"

I WAS WEAK. THE IDEA OF TRAVELING TO A WORMHOLE MADE ME ACT IRRATIONALLY, AND I WENT ALONG WITH THE PLAN. PLUS, I FIGURED GONZO WAS GOING TO NEED A SAFETY OFFICER FOR THE BIG STUNT IN THE VIDEO.

WAIT A MINUTE! GONZO IS HERE, TOO? JUST HOW MANY STOWAWAYS ARE ON THIS SHIP?

Suddenly, we heard strange voices hooting and hollering and saying "Weeeeeeeeee!" echoing down the hall. The sounds were coming from behind a big sliding door with a handmade paper sign taped to it.

"Wait just a minute," huffed Link. "That's not a virtual-reality ride. That's my man cave. Besides, don't these hooligans know it's a crime to impersonate a theme park?"

Kermit opened the sliding door, and we found Gonzo, Fozzie, and Animal inside buckled into chairs, staring out a window and hooting and hollering.

"Guuuuys!" Kermit flailed his arms. "What are you all doing in here?"

Rizzo fessed up. "It's not their fault. We told them this was a new virtual-reality motion ride. It was the only way to get them to stow away."

Kermit and I helped them undo their seat belts.

"AGAIN! AGAIN!" yelled Animal.

"Sorry, Animal," I said. "This isn't a virtual-reality ride. It's the real *Swinetrek*. That's a window you are looking out of, not a video screen."

"What the kid is trying to say is that presently, in reality, you are not actually experiencing virtual reality, you are actually present in our factual actuality. *Comprende?*" said Link.

"Thanks for clearing that up," First Mate Piggy snarked.

Fozzie looked around the room in total amazement. "So this isn't a carnival ride? No wonder I couldn't find any funnel cakes around here."

"Yeah," Kip admitted. "We totally pulled a fast one to get you guys on board with our new music-video idea. I sincerely hang my head in shame, yo."

ET TU, PASQUALE? ET TU? MY OWN SAFETY OFFICER. FOR SHAME! IF I WASN'T SO CONCERNED WITH STUNTS GOING HORRIBLY WRONG AND SUFFERING HORRIFIC INJURIES, I'D CONSIDER LETTING YOU GO.

I'M SORRY, GONZO.

"Well, right now we have to focus on getting to that wormhole," said Kermit.

Suddenly I felt a tugging on my pants leg. I looked down to see Curtis trying to get my attention. He started waving his arms and pointing down the hall again.

"Curtis? What is it, boy?" I asked, then I turned to the crew. "I think my rat might be picking up another scent trail."

"Another scent trail? This is ridiculous," huffed Piggy. She stomped her foot and shouted, "All right! If there are any other stowaways on this ship, show yourselves or face my shiny space boot!"

A loud *creeeak* came from above as a rusty ventilation duct grill swung open and two terrifying creatures peeked out...oh wait, it was just Statler and Waldorf.

"What are you two doing here?" asked Kermit. "You aren't in on this outer space music-video business, are you?"

HOWIE 5000's robot voice suddenly blared over the intercom. "All hands report to the bridge! I repeat, all hands report to the bridge! ASAP!"

"Come on, gang!" cried Link. "It could be an emergency! Follow me!"

AWWW, HOW CUTE. THE LITTLE RAT IS TRYING TO TELL YOU A JOKE, OKAY.

WHY DO YOU SAY THAT?

BECAUSE HE IS PULLING YOUR LEG, OKAY.

SQUEAK!

Sure enough, Curtis was, once again, tugging on my pants leg and pointing down the hall.

"Sorry, Curtis!" I said, scooping him up. "We've gotta go! I don't want that crazy computer upset with us."

Curtis squeaked in protest as I ran after the others.

On the bridge, HOWIE 5000 rolled out and addressed the stowaways. I was worried he was going to dispense some cruel punishment on the intruders. Boy, was I wrong.

"This is no joking matter!" HOWIE yelled, making everyone cower. "Now, in the meantime, band rehearsals will begin immediately."

"Band rehearsals?" I said.

"Yes," continued HOWIE. "The members of M.E.S.S. will convene in two minutes to rehearse a new musical number and accompanying stunt."

I was perplexed. "I thought you were supposed to give me math lessons so I won't flunk out of Eagle Talon Academy."

"Negative," HOWIE responded. "I have overrode Dr. Honeydew and Sam Eagle's orders. For the next twelve hours, you will do nothing but rehearse your new musical act and stunt spectacular."

"But HOWIE," Kermit interrupted, "we are here to get Danvers to the Wormhole N-1 and save humanity, not to perform pop songs."

HOWIE flared up, his lights blinking red. "Silence, fuzzy aquatic ringleader!"

YOU WILL COMPLY WITH MY ORDERS OR FACE A JOLT FROM MY UNCOMFO RAY! IT'S LIKE BEING TICKLED BY THREE THOUSAND JELLYFISH IN A VAT OF ANGRY FIRE ANTS!

"That definitely sounds uncomfortable!" Fozzie trembled.

"Trust me, it is!" said Gonzo. "That was my stunt at the *2005 Kids Pick Awards*."

Rizzo stepped up, nervously. "I hate to break it to you, Mr. 5000, but we don't even have all the members of M.E.S.S. with us. Scooter's not here. We couldn't trick him onto the ship because he's too smart to fall for such a cheap stunt."

"Heeeey!" snapped Fozzie.

"Uh, I mean, because he notoriously hates amusement park rides," Rizzo corrected himself.

"I accounted for this development," said HOWIE. "That is why I hog-tied and kidnapped Scooter before takeoff."

Suddenly, Dr. Strangepork jumped out from behind his computer console and zapped HOWIE 5000 with his stun laser! But the bolt bounced right off.

"Foolish spectacled science elder!" shouted HOWIE. "Traditional stun lasers have no effect on me! Now you shall pay the price!"

HOWIE released Dr. Strangepork from his beam and the doc slumped against the wall. "I'm okay!" he said with a cough.

"Whoa, yo!" Kip whispered in my ear. "I was all for doing a music video in space, but not if peeps are getting tied up and zapped."

"This HOWIE dude is straight up cuckoo-whack, yo!" said Cody.

"I've got one little question," Pasquale squeaked, bravely raising his hand.

"Speak, meek intellectual man-cub," said HOWIE.

"Why are you doing this?" Pasquale asked.

"Yeah, what does M.E.S.S. have to do with the wormhole and changing me back to my old self?" I echoed.

After our productive meeting on

the bridge, HOWIE 5000 gathered all the members of M.E.S.S. in the cafeteria. We slid the tables and chairs out of the way to make space for rehearsal.

For the next twelve hours we slaved away, dancing and singing and perfecting our act. HOWIE was a cruel taskmaster.

From now on, this dining area will be referred to as the M.E.S.S. Hall.

That's what it's called already, lunk head!

I KNEW that.

M.E.S.S. HALL

those dance grooves are unacceptable. Follow my lead. Watch my feet!

Dude, you don't have feet. You look like a rolling dishwasher.

I've been saving this for a special occasion. It's hair gel from the planet Suavemundo. It is five million times stronger than Earth products and can bond electromagnatrons to flibble-photons in seconds.

SPLOOT!

Uh... thanks, yo!

No pressure, Gonzo, but I expect the greatest stunt in history. Anything less and I will place you in a disintegration chamber!

Sounds like fun! But I can't work under this pressure! I don't even have access t real chickens!

After a day of nonstop dancing, singing, and stunt rehearsal, I was about to drop dead from exhaustion. Luckily, HOWIE gave us a two-minute-and-thirty-seven-second break.

I went and plopped down next to Pasquale.

Pasquale was being very quiet around me. I think he thought I was still miffed that he had stowed away on board, and I'll admit I was still a little shocked that he had gone along with the crowd. But I couldn't get too steamed at him. It was kind of cool having him along for the ride, and I was way too nervous about being transformed again to even worry about anything else.

"You know what?" I said. "I'm secretly really glad

you're here. I was afraid I'd missed my chance to say good-bye, just in case, you know, the trip through the wormhole doesn't go so well."

Pasquale let out a sigh of relief. "Whew! I was afraid you were still angry with me. And, hey, don't worry about that wormhole. It's not like it's going to turn you into ground hamburger meat or anything."

"Thanks for putting that image in my head, but it's not that I'm afraid of," I said. "I'm more afraid it will actually work as planned. What if, after I change back into a normal sixth grader, there's no more Muppet internship, no more being Gonzo's personal assistant, no more karate chops from Piggy? What if it's like nothing ever happened? What if I go through this wormhole and everything just goes back to the boring old way it used to be?"

Pasquale gave me a gentle punch on the arm. "The boring old way it used to be? You mean staying up late on weekends, watching hours and hours of Gonzo's greatest stunts, then reenacting them for the neighbors and getting thunderous applause— or at least imagining thunderous applause? Or memorizing every joke from *Fozzie Bear's Joke*

Encyclopedia and bombarding Mr. Piffle with a full-on pun joke assault? If going back to the boring old way it used to be is the worst thing that can happen, we're gonna be all right."

"I guess you've got a point," I said, chuckling. I was awfully glad Pasquale had stowed away.

Suddenly an alarm went off, and the ship started to sway like a listing sailboat.

Dr. Strangepork's voice called out over the intercom, "Attention! All hands on deck! All hands on deck!"

As I made my way to the exit, I experienced a strange sensation: My feet were moving, but they weren't touching the ground anymore. That's when everything around me started to float. Pasquale, Kip, Kermit—everyone and everything was rising toward the ceiling!

It was crazy being totally weightless. My canary-yellow hair was even wilder and more out-of-control than normal, floating above my head. Curtis drifted by me like a tiny rat astronaut out for a moonwalk.

We pulled ourselves along the walls all the way to the bridge, where the crew was battling to turn the ship hard right. The whole room was glowing green as the *Swinetrek* swayed and lurched.

"What's happening?" I yelled.

"Ve have arrived at the vormhole!" cried Dr. Strangepork. "Und I'm afraid we have gotten a little too close for comfort!"

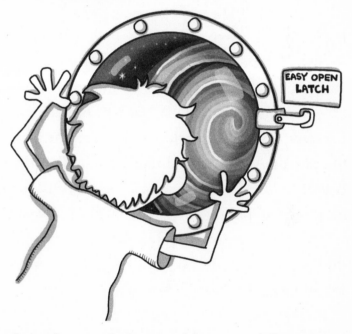

Through a porthole, I could see a swirling vortex, and it was giving off the same horrible green light that I had seen the night of my Muppetmorphosis!

"Why can't we pull out of it?" asked Kermit.

"But Doctor," said Piggy, looking at her console, "the plan was for us to stop just outside the wormhole, and then launch just Danvers through it. But for some reason, the flight has been reprogrammed to send the whole ship through, with all of us on board!"

"It was me!" shouted HOWIE 5000. "I altered the ship's course! We're all going through, and there's nothing you can do about it! If I were human, I would laugh maniacally right now!"

"How could you?" hissed Dr. Strangepork. Then he turned to us and screamed, "Hold on tight! Ve are going in!"

Everyone clutched one another as the ship plunged into the wormhole!

Here we go, I thought. This is the moment when everything changes back. Felt turns to flesh, feathers back to hair, tween Muppet superstar back to boring ol' sixth grader.

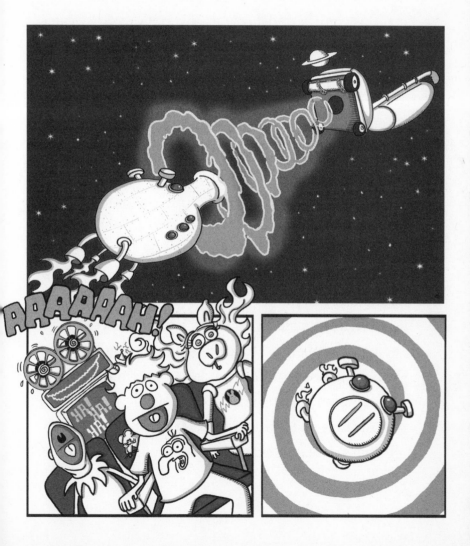

A huge, blinding flash of green filled the bridge, and then…nothing. Everything was quiet.

Once my eyes adjusted after the bright flash, I held my hands in front of my face, expecting to see my old pink flesh…but nothing had changed. I was still as orange and fuzzy as the Halloween sweater my grandma had knitted for me last fall.

"That's it?" Piggy shrugged, picking herself up off the floor. Everyone else got up, too. The gravity seemed to be working again, and the ship was no longer lurching.

Kermit and Pasquale and Gonzo helped me off the floor.

"Sorry, Danvers," said Kermit sadly. "Looks like it didn't work."

I slumped down in my seat. Curtis rubbed up against my neck.

"Well, Pasquale," I said with a sigh, "looks like I'm going to remain a Muppet for the rest of my days, which I guess won't be too long, since the world is teetering on the edge of destruction."

"At least we're in this together," said Pasquale.

That's when I heard a distant, deep thumping

sound. It was rhythmic, pulsing—like a drumbeat—
and it was coming from outside the ship.

We looked up at the video screen to see that we
were approaching a small planet, and the closer we
got, the louder the pulsing beat grew.

"We have arrived!" HOWIE 5000 cried with joy.

"Arrived where?" asked Piggy.

As we got closer to the planet, I saw a gigantic
stadium jutting up out of a crater in the center of
the lunar-landscape surface. The stadium looked
like it was packed with thousands of creatures.

HOWIE 5000 announced, "Welcome to the planet Koozebane, where we will compete in the *Universe's Got Chutzpah!* competition! Amateur acts from around the galaxy flock here every year to show their stuff and wow the judges!"

"Wait a minute," said Kermit. "You dragged us all the way out here to enter a talent show?"

"Not just any talent show. It is broadcast in over six hundred thousand different worlds, in five million languages!"

YOU MEAN NONE OF THIS HAD ANYTHING TO DO WITH MY MUPPETMORPHOSIS? WE DIDN'T EVEN HAVE TO COME TO THE WORMHOLE IN THE FIRST PLACE?

WAIT A MINUTE, YOU MEAN WE JUST READ A HUNDRED EIGHTY-SIX PAGES OF THIS BOOK FOR NOTHING?

THAT'S ALL RIGHT— I SLEPT THROUGH MOST OF THEM ANYWAY!

HOWIE explained his diabolical plan. "Weeks ago, when Dr. Honeydew assigned me to investigate your condition, he had me monitor the Wormhole N-1 with a telescope and listen for sound waves emanating from the region. That's when I picked up the interstellar broadcast of the *Universe's Got Chutzpah*! I watched one episode and was hooked! It had everything. Songs! Dancing! Three-headed acid-spitting alien poodles!"

"What does this have to do with us, yo?" asked Kip.

"When I first heard you and Danvers team up to form M.E.S.S. for that groovalicious 'Girl, Don't Be Rash,' I knew that you were good enough to win the competition. But I had to get you to the planet Koozebane first."

"So you fibbed to Dr. Honeydew about the sound of my music coming from the wormhole, and you made him think the green glow was somehow connected to my transformation," I said. "Very clever."

Pepe stepped up and put his foot down. "I'm sorry, okay. I am the band manager, and I cannot allow this unpaid performance in the talent contest. No way José, okay!"

YOU ARE NO LONGER THEIR MANAGER, SPINY ACCENTED CRUSTACEAN! I AM TAKING OVER FROM HERE ON OUT!

AND TO THAT I SAY CONGRATULATIONS! ENJOY YOUR NEW JOB. I'M GOING TO GO COWER IN THE CORNER, OKAY.

"But HOWIE," said Fozzie, "don't you care that the Earth is in danger?"

"It affects us not," HOWIE responded. "Because of me, you are all safe. No longer within range of a world bound for destruction!"

Kermit suddenly stepped up. "HOWIE! This is unacceptable! I demand that you turn this ship around and—"

HOWIE's lights went red and steam shot from his audio ports. "You will do as I say, pernicious amphibian! We will prove once and for all that M.E.S.S. is the greatest boy band in the galaxy, or I will turn you into frog gazpacho!"

"Ulp," Kermit said, gulping nervously. "Maybe we do have time for a quick performance."

"I'm so disappointed in you," I said to HOWIE. "I thought this wormhole was the key to solving the mystery of my Muppetmorphosis, but you used it to trick us."

HOWIE 5000 chuckled. "Forgive me, earthling Muppet-human hybrid, but the key to your Muppetmorphosis has been obvious since the second volume of your life story. Hee hee! Ha ha! Now, prepare to beam down to the surface, all of you! Hee hee!"

As HOWIE rolled away, laughing, Pasquale and I huddled. "He said the key to my Muppetmorphosis is in the second volume of my life story! That must mean book two. We have to find a copy of book two!"

"I didn't bring mine," said Pasquale. "Did anyone pack a copy in their luggage?"

SORRY. ALL I PACKED WAS THIS, OKAY.

YOU PACKED A LANTERN ON A LONG SPACE VOYAGE?

WHAT? THEY TOLD ME TO PACK *LIGHT*.

Dr. Strangepork pointed across the room. "I believe there is a copy over there. Link stands on it to make him look taller zan Piggy for press photos."

"How dare you!" cried Link. "That's top secret government info!"

"The truth hurts, muscle-brain!" snapped Piggy.

Pasquale ran over and snatched up the book and started poring over it. "I'll read it front to back 'til I solve the mystery!"

It was nerve-racking having a crazed computer following us with an Uncomfo Ray pointed at our backs.

"We've got to get back to the ship and return to Earth," I whispered to Kermit as we moved through the crowd. "We are wasting valuable time."

"I know," said Kermit. "But until we come up with a plan, we'd better just humor HOWIE."

"What is our plan, anyway, yo?" whispered Kip.

It was a good question. And I definitely did not know the answer. All I did know was that every second we wasted on this planet, the Earth was getting closer to destruction.

"Over here!" shouted HOWIE 5000 suddenly. "To enter the competition, we must first register our act."

We got in a huge line of aliens waiting to enter the contest. There was every kind of act you could imagine, and several you couldn't (we were on the planet Koozebane, after all).

Pasquale poked me on the shoulder. "Look behind us, dude. It looks like we're the last ones in line. We must have just made the cutoff to go for the big prize."

"Hey!" I said. "What is the prize if we win, anyway?"

HOWIE 5000 started rattling and whirring with excitement. "It's quite amazing, actually! If M.E.S.S. wins, the manager of the group—yours truly—gets an all-expenses-paid trip to the interstellar resort Venus Beach, plus a lifetime supply of keyboard wipes and a *Universe's Got Chutzpah!* T-shirt!"

"What about us, yo?" asked Kip. "We're the ones doing the singing and dangerous stunts."

"Oh, you will get the greatest prize of all," HOWIE said, chuckling. "The winners will be locked in a glass cage at the Koozebane zoo, where they will perform their hits for the rest of eternity or until they grow old and disintegrate, whichever comes first. It's quite an honor!"

"If that's what happens to the winners, I'm afraid to ask what happens if we lose," Fozzie said with a gulp.

"Failure is not tolerated," said HOWIE. "If all three judges buzz you, then you will be hit with a special laser that'll transform you into lime gelatin!"

"Lime gelatin?!" I cried.

"This is crazy, yo," wailed Kip. "If we win, we're forced to sing smooth jams for all eternity. If we lose, we're turned into a whack school-cafeteria dessert."

"I know! Isn't it terrific?" said Gonzo. "It's a win-win situation! I've always wanted to be transparent and citrus-flavored myself!"

"Okay, look, circuit-head," Piggy said to HOWIE. "These kids are amateurs. You need a professional, a true interstellar star of *moi's* celebritude to win this contest. Lucky for *vous*, I have prepared a fabulous routine. It's from the new musical *More Than You Can Bear*."

"Sorry," said HOWIE. "Your offer is honorable, brave diva pig creature, but you are no match for M.E.S.S. This crowd wants boy bands. They will tear out the seats, storm the stage, and declare total anarchy if they don't get their boy bands."

"Sounds like some of the sixth-grade girls at Coldrain," said Pasquale. "I guess some things are the same no matter where you go."

"*Sacre bleu!*" exclaimed Danny.

When we got to the front of the line, HOWIE 5000 made Scooter fill out the entry form for M.E.S.S.

While they were busy with that, I tried to brainstorm. *What to do? What to do?* I thought. My brain doesn't storm too well, especially under pressure.

Then I felt the tug at my pants leg again.

I looked down to see Curtis with a blank entry form in his mouth and a pencil in his tail.

"What is it, boy? Do you want to enter the contest, too?"

"Maybe your rat has hidden talents, yo," cried Kip. "He's secretly a little rodent heartthrob. Maybe he can go on so we don't have to, yo!"

"Settle down, yo," I said. "I think he's trying to tell us something."

Curtis squeaked and looked over at HOWIE, then back at me. Suddenly, I felt like I was on Curtis's wavelength. I was thinking like a rat. A plan was dawning on me. I grabbed the entry form from Curtis and started scribbling on it, praying HOWIE wouldn't see me.

OKAY, GUYS. THERE'S BEEN A CHANGE IN PLANS. PIGGY, WE NEED YOUR HELP WITH THE ACT AFTER ALL. AND LINK, DO YOU HAVE ANY MORE OF THAT SPECIAL MUD YOU USE FOR A FACE MASK?

WHY? THAT STUFF COSTS THIRTY DOLLARS PER OUNCE.

OH, PUH-LEASE! YOU GOT IT FOR FREE OFF ZE GROUND!

While we waited for our turn to go on, there was a really bad extraterrestrial magician on the stage pulling a Snoofblorgh out of a hat. I could hear the audience booing and shouting. The poor guy was bombing big-time. That's when I heard three loud buzzes, then a high-pitched *zap*! accompanied by a blinding lime-green flash. The audience erupted in a thunderous burst of applause and cheers as the poor magician was wheeled off the stage, right in front of us. He had gotten the green-gelatin treatment!

Then it was our turn to hit the stage, and I was a nervous wreck!

"Don't be afraid," Pasquale comforted me. "Maybe being gelatin will be easier than being a Muppet. You'll certainly be a lot jigglier, and you'll smell nice and fruity."

"You're not helping," I said. "Just make sure Gonzo is ready for our big stunt."

Kermit gave us a pep talk before we went on. "All right, break a leg out there! And remember, it's not about whether you win or lose, it's about having a good time. So don't let the threat of being transformed into a quivering, gelatinous blob spoil your fun!"

"That wasn't very comforting," whimpered Fozzie.

We rushed out onto the stage and strapped on our instruments. Animal started a slow drumroll as the lights came up. Scooter, Fozzie, Cody, and Danny were in their dance positions, and Kip was ready at his guitar. I was playing a Skookilanjo. That's a famous Koozebanian instrument that's like a cross between a banjo and Skookiluniper—whatever that is.

For the first time, I got a good look at the judges. They were a menacing bunch.

The crowd gave us a big round of applause as Kermit ran out to give us a proper introduction. "Ladies and gentle—uh, whatevers! We've traveled from over a million miles away, mostly against our will, to make a big M.E.S.S. on your stage! Let's give a great big hand, and maybe a tentacle or two, for M.E.S.S.! Yaaaaay!!!"

Kip stepped up to the mic to address the thousands of folks in the audience. He had even learned some Koozebanian for the occasion.

The crowd went nuts. I had no idea what he said, but I'm sure it was nauseatingly smooth.

I strummed my Skookilanjo and belted out the first note of the song

Kip had written especially for our outer-space gig. We rocked the house!

The song was going over like gangbusters! We were melting the hearts of every tween girl in the audience—even the Pookblurps, who reportedly have five hearts. The crowd was going nuts, and the judges, so far, had not hit their buzzers.

M.E.S.S. presents
Step to My Neptune

Step to my Neptune.
Hale-Bop 'til you drop!

Step to my Neptune.
This beat, it just won't stop!

Girl, I got more bling than Saturn's rings
Shakin' my moon buggy booty
like it ain't no thing.

I don't wanna hear no jive,
Cuz this dancing machine's
goin' into hyperdrive.

Now, save the drama for Andromeda,
and if you're lucky
I'll cut a rug for ya.

This ain't no interstellar cruise,
If you challenge my beats,
get ready to lose.

Step to my Neptune.
Do the Galactic Slide
to the side.

Step to my Neptune.
From my skills
you cannot hide!

Shake it!
Shake it!

This one's called
The Milky-Wave!
Wocka! Wocka!

Scratch! Scratch!

I'm doing the robot!

I find that deeply offensive!

The crowd went silent and, for a second, I was nervous that the judges would buzz us since Piggy didn't come back. But instead, the audience went wild! The judges loved it, too! They gave M.E.S.S. a score of 3.333339998888876 Kookenzingerpointz, which is apparently pretty good. In fact, we were in the lead!

HUGGA WUGGA!

THAT WAS THE GREATEST DISPLAY OF SHOWMANSHIP SINCE THE GALLEY-OH-HOOP-HOOP IN SEASON ONE!

EH! I'VE SEEN BETTER.

"Wow! It looks like we may actually win this thing, guys," said Kermit.

"Oh, no," cried Fozzie. "If we win, we have to perform that song for all eternity in the zoo! I think I might just rather get turned into gelatin."

"Don't worry," I whispered. "It's not over yet."

An announcer came over the loudspeaker and said, "And now, folks, we have just one more contestant!"

"That's funny," said HOWIE 5000. "I could have sworn we were the last act to perform."

"Ladies and gentlemen!" the voice announced. "Our final performer, from the planet Earth… HOWIE 5000, the Supercomputer Comedian!!!"

HOWIE 5000 rolled out to the center of the stage, where a bright spotlight hit him. The crowd went silent, waiting for his first joke. You could hear crickets chirping.

"Uh…thank you! Thank you!" he whimpered. "Uh…I'm a little nervous. You'll have to excuse me."

"Tell a joke, for Pete's sake!" shouted George the Janitor.

HOWIE had gotten three buzzes! A laser cannon slowly rose up from behind the judges.

"No! Please!" pleaded HOWIE. "I have a wife and three small laptops at home!" The cannon fired out a blobby green burst of light.

When the smoke cleared, the audience cheered and clapped, and HOWIE 5000 oozed over to us.

Set a course for Earth, Link!"
said Kermit. "We've been out here too long."

With everyone back on board the *Swinetrek*, there was a sense of great relief.

"Thank goodness that cuckoo CPU is not flying zis ship anymore!" said Dr. Strangepork. "But it is too bad he vas turned into gelatin."

"Yeah," said Fozzie. "I guess he got his just *desserts*. Wocka! Wocka!"

Kermit stood up and announced, "Well, I just want to thank Piggy and Danvers and Gonzo for their bravery and ingenuity in helping us escape."

THANKS, KERMIT. I FEEL I STRETCHED MYSELF IN WAYS I NEVER HAVE BEFORE, AND I'VE REALLY GROWN AS A PERFORMER.

"What about *mon capitan?*" complained Link. "Don't I get any thanks?"

"You didn't lift a finger to help us," Piggy pointed out.

"I'll have you know I strained my finger pressing the DISTRESS CALL button on my walkie-talkie. I can hardly be expected to lift it."

Pasquale and Kip thanked me as well. "It was really clever how you entered HOWIE 5000 in the competition," said Pasquale. "Smart thinking."

MES HÉROS FANTASTIQUES!

YEAH, IT WAS INGENIOUS, DUDE. I NEVER COULD HAVE THOUGHT UP SOMETHING SO CLEVER AND...UH, I LOST MY TRAIN OF THOUGHT, YO.

DON'T THANK ME. IT WAS CURTIS WHO CAME UP WITH THE WHOLE SCHEME!

Despite having survived our escapade, I was still bummed. We had traveled to the depths of space and really weren't any closer to solving the mystery of my Muppetmorphosis or saving the planet.

"I just can't believe we wasted so much time," I said with a sigh.

"I'm afraid I must take some responsibility for that," said Dr. Strangepork. "I took HOWIE 5000 at his vord. Little did I know he vas, to put it in scientific terms, crazy in ze coconut!"

I looked over at Pasquale. He was still flipping through book two, looking for clues. "I just know the answer is in here somewhere!" he said.

Suddenly, Curtis started squeaking and waving at me again.

LOOK! I THINK CURTIS MAY HAVE PICKED UP ON THE SCENT OF ANOTHER STOWAWAY!

ALL THESE STOWAWAYS ARE SUCKING UP THE SHIP'S OXYGEN!

WORRIED THEY'RE STEALING YOUR JOB?

Dr. Strangepork pulled out his sensor again, and it immediately started bleeping and buzzing. "The rat is right! I am picking up another life-form in the vicinity of the cryogenic hibernation chamber on level three!"

"I'll lead the way!" Fozzie volunteered. "If there's anything I know, it's hibernation. Let's go!"

We crept our way slowly down the corridor toward the cryogenic room. Our nerves were on edge.

"What if it's HOWIE 5000?" Link shivered. "Returned as a gelatinous bloblike creature to smother us in our sleep?"

"Just remain calm," said Dr. Strangepork as he opened the doors to the room, and we slinked in. There was a thin layer of fog flowing over the floor like swamp gas.

I could see a big hibernation chamber at the far side of the room, and it looked like there was a figure inside—a pint-size, pinkish, humanoid figure. Whatever it was, it was frozen solid in a huge block of ice.

I couldn't believe it! My irritating sister had been on the *Swinetrek* the whole time. That's what my parents must have been trying to tell me from mission control.

"What's that brat—I mean, that little angel—doing on board?" asked Miss Piggy.

"My thoughts exactly," I said. "Chloe! What the heck are you doing on the *Swinetrek*? And how did you get in here?"

"I snuck on board the bus when it came to pick you up, then I made my way onto the *Swinetrek* to twy to stop the launch," Chloe said. "But I got distwacted by that box of Fudgesicles on the top shelf of the cwyogenic chamber. Curse you, Fudgesicles! You will be the death of me someday! When I was in the chamber, somebody must have pushed the START button, and I got fwozen solid."

"It must have been HOWIE 5000," said Pasquale. "He didn't want anything interfering with the launch."

"Who's HOWIE 5000?" asked Chloe.

"An awful, manipulative, evil, controlling robot obsessed with fame," I said. "You would have gotten along with him great."

"Anyway," Chloe continued, "you don't have to go to space! I know for a fact that the wormhole thingy had nothing to do with your twansformation!"

"Uh, we kinda figured that out," I said. "The hard way. But how did you know? And stop it with the fake cutesy accent!"

"Because...I...I'm the reason you transformed," she confessed. "The day before your transformation, I used my birthday wish to wish you'd turn into a Muppet."

I didn't know whether to be mad or laugh uncontrollably.

"Er—what?" was all I could get out.

"It's true!" said Pasquale, pointing at his book. "It's right here in book two, chapter eight, page seventy-six! Chloe made a secret birthday wish just twenty-four hours before your Muppetmorphosis."

"Why would you use up your birthday wish to turn me into a Muppet?" I scoffed.

"Because it's all you ever talked about," Chloe said. "Gonzo this and Gonzo that. What would Gonzo say? I wish I were like Gonzo. I wish I was a Muppet. Muppets. Muppets. Muppets!"

"So I'm supposed to believe that you were actually trying to do something nice for me? Yeah, right."

SORT OF. I ALSO REALLY WANTED TO SEE WHAT YOU WOULD LOOK LIKE WITH A REMOVABLE NOSE AND FLIP-TOP MOUTH. IT'S KIND OF AWESOME.

"I'm glad you are being honest, Chloe," said Kermit, "but there's really no way a birthday wish can come true like that. So don't blame yourself."

"This wasn't just any birthday wish," replied Chloe. "There was a highly sophisticated, high-tech scientific device involved."

Chloe whipped out a secret file with a picture on

it. "This is the device: the Birthday Wish Special Edition Fluffleberry!"

Everyone screamed.

"Oh, *dios mio*! It's horrible, okay!" screamed Pepe.

"Only three of them were ever made," Chloe continued. "According to their commercials, the doll used the latest technology to grant three wishes. I got mine because I collected over two thousand proofs of purchase from Fluffleberry Frosted Sugar Cubes cereal."

"No wonder she's hyper," said Piggy.

"The trouble all started the night before Danvers turned into a Muppet," Chloe began....

225

"So explain why you stole Danvers's nose," said Pasquale.

"Well," said Chloe, "once I found the Birthday Wish Fluffleberry, I was gonna use one of the other wishes to turn the Muppet nose back to the way it used to be, just to see if it would work."

"Ew." I grimaced. "You were gonna walk around with my severed nose in your pocket?"

"Yeah, didn't think that through," admitted Chloe. "It would have stained my dress."

"Why didn't you tell me this before we got on the ship?" I yelled.

"Ha!" laughed Chloe. "Like you would have listened, Mr. I-won't-share-a-room-with-a-felon."

I *had* been pretty hard on the little devil ever since she got busted. "Sorry about that," I said, looking down. "But, how do we reverse the wish?"

"If we can find that doll," Chloe said, "it has two more wishes on it. We can use another wish to turn you back into the normal, boring, slightly wimpy, unpopular boy you once were, and the last wish to stop the destruction of our world."

"I guess my first question is why did the Fluffleberry

doll get recalled in the first place?" asked Kermit.

Chloe looked at the crew of the *Swinetrek* and said, "Why don't you ask the man who helped create it—one Dr. Julius Strangepork!"

All eyes darted to the good doctor. My mouth fell open.

"Yes! Yes! I admit it! It vas me!" he cried. "But I had no idea it had anything to do vith the destruction of our planet, honest!"

"Ve designed it to bring joy," said Dr. Strangepork. "The doll would send out positively charged Hoggs-Bacon particles designed to grant the simple vishes of a child. There vere three prototypes that went out to children who collected the most proofs of purchase. After the first boy made his first wish, something vent horribly wrong, so ve recalled the other dolls und ordered that they be destroyed."

"What went wrong?" asked Gonzo.

"He vished for a lifetime supply of rocky road ice cream," said Dr. Strangepork.

"What's so bad about that?" asked Piggy. "Sounds like heaven on Earth."

"He got his vish. All at once. It landed on his head. Thirteen tons of rocky road. Vith real rocks!"

"Sheesh!" Kermit grimaced.

"Ve realized that the vishes brought unforeseen circumstances, so the dolls had to be confiscated und incinerated. Once ve destroyed that doll, the effects of the ice cream vent away, although the boy is three inches shorter than he used to be."

"Why can't we just use up another wish to reverse the problem?" I asked.

"No," said Strangepork. "Each vish, even one to restore order, sets off a chain reaction of unpredictable calamity. The doll must be destroyed!"

"For some reason, they are holding on to my doll. Somewhere in the Fluffleberry headquarters, it is still lying around," said Chloe. "If we can destroy it, your Muppetmorphosis will be lifted, and the world will return to its normal, worry-free, peaceful ways."

BUT HOW IN THE WORLD ARE WE GONNA BREAK INTO FLUFFLEBERRY HEADQUARTERS? THAT PLACE IS LIKE FORT KNOX!

HELLO? WE HAVE A SPACESHIP EQUIPPED WITH A TRANSPORKER BEAM!

SET A COURSE FOR FLUFFLE INC.! AND IN THE MEANTIME, SET THE TABLE FOR A FOUR-COURSE MEAL. I'M FAMISHED!

The *Swinetrek* hurtled back toward Earth at Warp 3. Dr. Strangepork had set a course for the exact coordinates of the Fluffleberry headquarters. As we approached home, I noticed that the planet looked really different.

"Look!" said Pasquale. "The Earth is all wonky!"

It was like the planet's surface was made out of felt, and it was rolling and bulging as if the Earth was filled with churning liquid.

Suddenly, we picked up a signal from mission control on the video screen.

It was Dr. Honeydew, and he was sending out an SOS!

ATTENTION, *SWINETREK*. IF YOU CAN HEAR THIS MESSAGE, TURN BACK! STAY AWAY FROM THE PLANET EARTH. IT HAS BEEN OVERRUN WITH BEAKER CLONES, VIOLENT TREMORS ARE SHAKING THE PLANET, DOGS AND CATS HAVE DECLARED A TRUCE, BOYS ARE FLOCKING TO ROMANTIC COMEDIES—THINGS ARE ABSOLUTELY CRAZYBOBBLES!

"Ahoy, Doc!" announced Kermit, once again wearing his *Muppet Treasure Island* captain's hat. "Don't give up hope just yet! Come on, crew! Batten down the hatches!"

It was weird. The closer we got to Earth, the more everyone started reverting to previous acting roles. Kermit and Fozzie were acting like seafaring swashbucklers again. Then Gonzo and Rizzo ran out in their *Muppet Christmas Carol* outfits.

It seemed like everyone was losing their grasp on reality!

The ship was descending into chaos. I had to do something!

"EVERYBODY, GET A GRIP!" I screamed. "Look, people! I need you to hold on to reality for just a little while longer! The fate of the world rests in our hands. Just stay with me. I need you guys. Now more than ever."

Kermit took off his captain's hat and rubbed his eyes. "Danvers is right. We have to hold it together. We're so close."

"Actually, we're too close!" screamed Link. "Brace for impact!!!"

We assembled outside the ship and made our way through the dark halls of Fluffle Inc. Smoke and explosions and screams filled the air as the earth rumbled and rolled beneath our feet.

We rounded a corner and came upon a team of security guys. "Uh-oh! Security!" I yelled to the others. "We can't let ourselves get captured!"

But capturing us was the last thing on their minds.

Then we saw attorney Finn Kontempt running down the hall, looking frantic and lost.

"Hey!" I yelled. "It's that lawyer who kicked you off the Fluffleberry movie, Chloe!"

"Zap him!" Chloe ordered.

Miss Piggy pointed her space zapper at the lawyer.

"No! We're not here to zap anybody!" I said. I grabbed the lawyer and pleaded with him. "We have to destroy the last Birthday Wish Fluffleberry, or the world is going to end! Where do they keep it?"

Dr. Strangepork went up to the door and used his electro-code cracking device to try to open it. "I hope you guys brought a good book. It may take me several hours to crack ze lock."

"Oh, brother!" Piggy said with a sigh, reaching over and pushing a big button next to the door that said OPEN.

The door opened slowly and I could see a huge lab full of jars and test tubes and scientific equipment. The ceiling was fifty feet high and made of fortified steel beams. At the far side of the room, way up high, the Birthday Wish Fluffleberry was sitting in a display case, smiling down on us. In between us and the doll was an army of windup Fluffleberries, and they were waddling slowly toward us, all with crazy bug eyes and babbling "Goo goo! Ga ga!"

"This will forever live in my nightmares, yo," said Kip.

242

I woke up to see Gonzo posters on the ceiling staring down at me. I was back in my own bedroom. Chloe was in the bunk bed beneath mine, snoring like a water buffalo, and Curtis was curled up next to me. With a yawn, I sat up in bed. Curtis smacked his lips and stretched, then took a look at me.

Curtis let out a squeak of terror when he saw me. "What is it, boy?" I said, reaching out to pet him. That's when I noticed my arm was strangely fleshy. Almost a pinkish color.

I made my way down the bunk-bed ladder, past Chloe, and then I walked across the floor to the bathroom. I noticed that my legs seemed sturdier than usual, and when I grabbed the doorknob, I found that it was super easy to turn. I flipped on the bathroom light and looked in the mirror to find...

The old Danvers was back! My condition was fully reversed!

I was so happy I could barely contain myself. I looked over to see Curtis staring at me from the doorway.

"Wait a minute!" I paused, suddenly scared. "Surely this wasn't all a dream? The readers will wanna kill me if it was all just a dream."

At that moment, a groggy Chloe walked in and took one look at me and said...

I was beyond relieved. "So it wasn't all a dream? I really did transform and the world almost ended?"

"Yep! And I'm sorry I turned you into a Muppet!" Chloe sniffled. "Next time, I'll use my birthday wish for something selfish, like unimaginable wealth or all-you-can-eat fro-yo for the rest of my life!"

There was a knock at the door.

Chloe pushed me aside and wiped away her tears.

I opened the door and found my parents standing there in the hall, stunned. They swept me up in a huge hug.

"You're back?" my mom said, beaming.

"Lookin' good, sport," said my dad. "Good to see you've put some meat on those bones."

It was the first time I had seen my parents that happy in a long time.

They showered me with attention and praise all morning. Mom even made me a special breakfast meat loaf with an egg-yolk center. She really shouldn't have.

I took a look outside and saw a mob of reporters waiting by the front door.

"They've been out there ever since you launched

into space," said my mom. "Everybody wants an interview with the first kid in space."

"Not to mention the savior of the planet," added my dad.

"Yikes!" I said, grabbing my bike gear. "I wanna go over to Pasquale's house, but I'll never get past all these reporters."

"Leave it to me!" said Chloe.

"All intwaviews must be scheduled thwough me, people!" announced Chloe.

While she distracted the press, I biked my way over to Pasquale's house at the speed of a certain pig-shaped rocket. When I got there, he was already running out to greet me.

"It happened! It really happened!" he yelled as he gave me a hearty hug. "It's good to have you back! Although I'm going to miss being able to snatch your nose off your face and hide it while you're sleeping."

I AM GONNA MISS MY FLIP-TOP MOUTH. IT WAS COOL BEING ABLE TO READ THE LABEL ON THE BACK OF MY JEANS WITHOUT TURNING MY HEAD.

Suddenly, I went from happy to a little gloomy. "Do you think Gonzo and Kermit and the guys will even remember me?" I asked Pasquale. "Do we still have internships?"

"Let's go find out!" said Pasquale, grabbing his bike. We pedaled over to the Muppet Theater, only to find…the Hazy Film Theater?

"It's gone," I said. I was destroyed. Maybe it *was* all a dream.

Pasquale tried to stay positive. "Let's go check Eagle Talon Academy," he said.

We zoomed over to Sam's school…but it was just a run-down government building. "I guess it's back to Coldrain Middle School for me," I said with a sigh.

Next we tried Rowlf's Veterinarian's Hospital, but it was a strip mall.

"You see? The Muppets are gone," I said, sighing again. "They're in Hollywood, where they belong. They've never heard of me."

"Hey," said Pasquale. "If I remember it, and everyone else remembers it, surely Kermit and the gang do, too."

We sat on the concrete steps near the strip mall, slurping on a couple of Splershies. But not even the feeling of Extreme Mango Citrus dissolving my tongue could cheer me up.

That night, Pasquale and I tried to forget our troubles by pigging out on Cheezy-Q's and watching some seriously disgusting zombie movies. But even the ripping of zombie flesh couldn't pull me out of my funk. Speaking of ripping, Chloe was making a lot of racket tearing her Fluffleberry posters off the walls.

I'VE COME TO THE CONCLUSION THAT FLUFFLEBERRIES REALLY JUST FREAK ME OUT. TOMORROW, WE'RE HAVING A BONFIRE. BRING MARSHMALLOWS!

Mom and Dad knocked on the door and leaned in with a pizza. "We've got a Monster Martian Mangia Special from Pepperoni Planet," said my dad. "And did one of you order southern fried shrimp?"

"Southern fried shrimp?" I said, confused. "I don't think so."

GIDDYUP, LITTLE DOGS, OKAY! YEE-HAW! AND TELL YOUR DADDY HERE THAT I AM A KING PRAWN, NOT A SHRIMP, OKAY.

"Pepe!" I cried. I rushed to hug the little stinker.

"Watch the antennae, okay," said Pepe. "I want to look good for the lady prawns."

"How did you get here?" asked Pasquale.

"I caught a ride with a bear and a pig and the frog and the...whatever, too."

I have to admit, I was a little shocked they hadn't mentioned that I'd transformed back into a normal kid. "Soooo…you guys don't care that I am no longer actually a Muppet?"

Gonzo looked me over. "Well, come to think of it, you do look a little freaky. But I think you qualify as an honorary Muppet."

"Yes," Pepe said, nodding. "You have the brain of a Muppet, and that is all that is counted, okay."

"I'm not sure if that's a compliment or not," I said, "but I accept!"

Fozzie looked really excited. "Kermit, should we tell them about our amazing idea, too?"

"I don't see why not," Kermit said.

WE WANNA MAKE A MOVIE ABOUT WHAT HAPPENED! HERE'S THE PITCH: NORMAL SIXTH-GRADE BOY GOES TO SLEEP ONE NIGHT, WAKES UP A MUPPET, GETS A GIG AT THE MUPPET THEATER, BECOMES A BOY-BAND SINGER, FIGHTS GIANT RATS, ZOMBIE COMEDIANS, AND A NINE-FOOT CHICKEN, AND TRAVELS TO THE FAR SIDE OF THE GALAXY! JUST IMAGINE IT!

HE DOESN'T HAVE TO IMAGINE IT, FOZZIE—HE LIVED IT.

OH, RIGHT.

I was dumbstruck. "Seriously? You guys want to

make a movie about my adventures as a Muppet?"

"We're serious as can be," Kermit said, nodding.
"We've already sent a script to several big Hollywood
producers, and they're just dying to produce it! Of
course, it'll take some serious special effects to turn
you into a Muppet since we don't have anymore
Fluffleberries to fall back on."

I couldn't believe it.

I was on cloud nine, when all of a sudden...

A bright green light flashed in the window!

"What was that?" asked Gonzo.

I walked over to the window. "Wow, I had totally
forgotten about the green flash. We never figured
out what the heck it had to do with my Muppetmorphosis."

It flashed again!

We crept down the stairs and stepped out into the warm night. Another green flash caught our attention. It was coming from around the corner. We all made our way down the sidewalk, following the flashing green flicker.

Pepe stopped in his tracks and sniffed the air. "Listen," he cried. "I smell the aroma of burnt pistachios and green apples, okay!"

He was right! I could smell it, too. It reminded me of the night of my transformation. I had smelled the very same thing.

We followed the flashing light and the smell.

As we rounded the bend, we came upon an old diner with a big green neon sign. The sign was on the fritz and was flashing brightly every few minutes with a buzzing sound. A couple of big clumsy moths were humming around the neon, slamming into each other like bumper cars.

"That's it?" Piggy shrugged. "All that mystery over the flashing green light and it was a busted neon sign?"

"I hadn't even thought about this place," Pasquale said, laughing.

"It was right over our noses the whole time," said Gonzo.

"I feel so silly," I said. "So the green light had absolutely nothing to do with anything!"

"Hey, if it wasn't for that green light, we would never have gotten the all-expenses-free trip to the Wormhole and zapped in the *cabeza* by a crazy computer, okay!" Pepe added.

"Well, as long as we're here," said Kermit, "how about a slice of pie on me?"

"I'd rather have it on a plate, Kermit," Fozzie said with a smile. "Wocka! Wocka!"

Inside, we piled into a big booth near the window. The place was an old-school greasy spoon—just the way I like it.

"I'll just have a smoothie," said Piggy. "*Moi* is watching her figure."

Chloe slapped her menu down. "To heck with that! I'm having the triple-decker super-fudge-sludge sundae!"

"Oh…what the hey!" Piggy caved in. "*Moi* will have one of those, too! With two-percent whipped cream, of course."

"This place isn't half bad," said Pasquale. "Maybe I'll bring Sofi here on our first date instead of Pepperoni Planet."

"It'll probably be easier to impress her with chocolate over greasy cheese and sausage," I said, nodding.

"And look here!" said Kermit. "They have burnt pistachio and apple pie! That explains the scent!"

Gonzo was enjoying some cake when he suddenly blurted out, "That reminds me, guys! I've got a new stunt I need your help with. I want to be baked into a giant brownie at 450 degrees, then eat my way out while Camilla plays the kazoo."

As I slurped a milkshake, I figured I was about the happiest former Muppet on the planet. "You know what, Kermit? This is the life."

Kermit smiled. "Yep. We'll all have to get together here more often."

Pepe suddenly shouted, "*Ay, caramba!* We forgot about the others!" He ran to the door and yelled out, "Come on in, everybody!"

The front doors opened like a floodgate and the place was overrun with Muppets. Dr. Teeth and The Electric Mayhem Band, Rowlf, Chef, Sam Eagle, Dr. Honeydew and Beaker, Link and Strangepork, Statler and Waldorf, Beauregard...everyone was there!

Kermit looked over at me and grimaced. "Well, maybe not too often."

As the diner filled up with fur, felt, and feathers, Pasquale leaned in toward me. "I bet, secretly, you're gonna miss being a Muppet."

I laughed and took a mighty slurp of my chocolate shake. "You know, Pasquale," I said, "the one thing I've learned from this experience is that a Muppet-morphosis is a lot like a bus that won't back up."

"How so?" he asked.

"It's irreversible."

KIRK SCROGGS's literary career began in 1912 with a job writing wrappers for the Sacre Blew! Bubblegum company. His famous line, "Naturally Delicious, Artificially Flavored," was praised by famed critic, Madame Zelda Rose, who called it, "short, but sweet." During the war, Kirk teamed with top military mind, Sam Eagle, to pen his patriotic *Pull Yourself Up by Your Bootstraps* speech. Who could forget Sam's immortal words, "Ra Ra, ra ra rahh. Ga Ga, ooh la la!"? Recently, Mr. Scroggs released his masterwork, *The Monster Book of Creature Features*. When asked what they thought of it in a *NY Tribune* interview, renowned critics Statler and Waldorf replied, "We couldn't put that book down!" When asked why, they responded, "Because it's glued to our hands!" Then they proceed to laugh and barrage the interviewer with cheap insults.

READ THE ENTIRE SERIES!

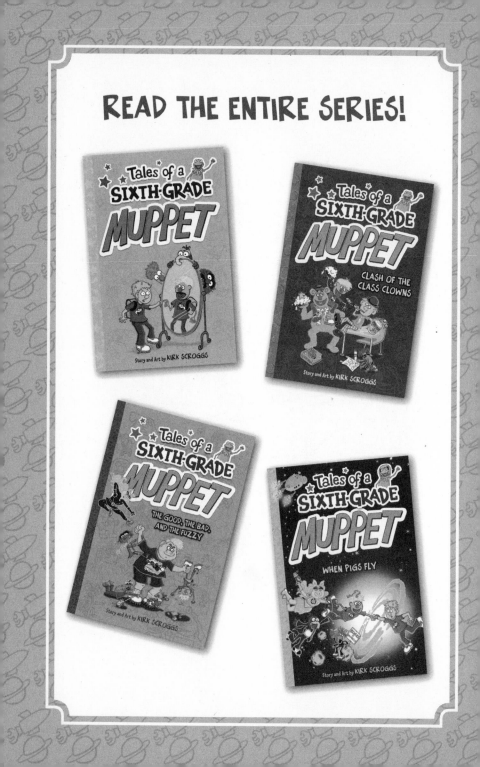